THE MERCENARY

A WARREN PARISH STORY

A STANDALONE FROM THE SOUL SUMMONER SERIES

ELICIA HYDER

For More Information:
www.eliciahyder.com

For our military family.

THE SOUL SUMMONER SERIES

ONE

September 2008
Somewhere outside Baghdad, Iraq

I'm going to save the world.

That was the kind of bass-ackwards thinking that sent me to this hellhole in the first place. I'd like to say I wound up behind the scope of an M40 for a more noble reason like honor or duty to God and country, but I didn't.

Wanna hear the truth? The

overwhelming majority of men I've served with in the military enlisted for one of two reasons: to save the world and to blow shit up.

And despite all the ways I am not an average grunt, in this, I am absolutely no different.

Like most of us, I signed away my life and body because of a misguided idea that somehow I would endear myself to mankind one round at a time. In reality, it was nothing more than a superhero-wannabe's delusion. Psychobabble bullshit they feed you at the recruiting office as you stand there with a pen between your uncalloused, trigger-happy fingers.

Nobody gets to save the world.

And nobody, sure as hell, earns any kind of endearment.

But the blowing shit up part never gets old.

Six years and five combat-zone tours later, I still hear phantom M67s detonate in my sleep and crave the smell of burning comp-B and C-4. A side of me—the side I don't talk about with anyone outside the brotherhood—lives for the controlled chaos that accompanies detonation.

The mess.

The destruction.

The high.

There's nothing better.

Pending use of explosives was the only upside to our current position: a ghostly village ripe with IEDs outside Baghdad.

A stray dog was feasting on a rotting carcass in the dead center of the dirt road up ahead. Our Humvee slowed to a crawl.

"Is it human?" one of the guys in the back asked.

I strained my eyes as I focused on the lifeless heap. "Nah, roadkill."

My sixth sense knew the difference between animal remains and human. The guys were beginning to trust my bizarre intuition, even if it secretly scared the shit out of them.

Sergeant Brayden Burch, my assistant team leader, looked over at me from behind the wheel. "Keep going?"

I nodded. "If it was a bomb, the mutt would be dead." We rolled past the dog, who couldn't be bothered to pull its bloody snout from the putrid snack to acknowledge us.

It was 0400 hours, and I was crammed six men deep in a Humvee built for five. We were all doing the exact same thing: visually combing every building and alleyway along the road through our night vision goggles. Carefully inspecting each rock in the dust and every crack in the dry earth because the slightest irregular detail could be a death sentence.

Even without the direct heat of the sun, the Humvee was an oven, an oven that smelled like ass and explosives. In the war-torn Middle East, the scent and sound of guns, ammo, and grenades knocking around was a sensory salve to our frayed nerves, reassuring us that if things went sideways and we came under fire, we were prepared.

And the probability of attack was high despite that the war in Iraq was fizzling to a close. Most of the US military had gone home or back to Afghanistan, and I had expected we'd be deployed there. Instead, we were sent to squash a small but fierce insurgent cell that had risen out of the ashes of the Triangle of Death, just south of Baghdad.

These days, the Islamic Jihad State (IJS) made the trek through the northeastern part of the country one of the most dangerous commutes in the world.

They'd already opened fire on us once. Thankfully, the only casualty had been one of our five Humvees. Cause of death? A bullet spray to the radiator. Command had ordered us to destroy it and get the heck out of there. We listened.

While their militia was busy tearing up Sadr City behind us, we were to find and destroy a weapons cache rumored to be in an abandoned factory just south of the city of Tuz Sehir. Our mission was simple: blow their shit up.

Hell yeah.

The passenger-side wheels caught a pothole, and my helmet banged against the bulletproof glass. In the middle of the two back seats, sitting cross-legged on a metal shelf meant for storing gear, Sergeant Chaz McKenna swore and braced himself against the ceiling of the vehicle. "This is bullshit. I'm going to die of a concussion before I have the chance to get shot or blown up."

"Quit whining, Chaz. You know you like riding bitch," Earp, a rifleman, said behind me.

I suppressed a smile. It was a little funny to see McKenna getting knocked around in the back of my Humvee. Even though he was a team leader like me, in my car, he had no authority. "Don't worry. We'll get your team a new ride once we get back to base. This is only temporary."

"Great. Then at least I'll die out here without a charley horse," Chaz grumbled.

We pushed on down the road with hopefully nothing but sand and camel spiders between us and a few hours rest.

"Two more klicks to the Hilton, boys," Burch said.

I glanced back over my shoulder through

the small space between the legs of our machine gunner in the turret. Through the bit of back window I could see, the horizon appeared calm. Before I turned back around, the flash of a mortar illuminated the buildings in the distance. "Only two klicks?" I asked, wondering if roughly a mile and a half would be far enough from the action to actually rest.

"That's the word from Hammerhead," Chaz said. "He *says* this area's already been cleared and that we're beyond their reach."

A collective groan rose above the racket of the engine.

A retired master sergeant once told me, "The deadliest man on the battlefield is an officer with a radio and a map." The joke was certainly true of the guy making decisions for us, Major Benjamin Calvin, call sign Hammerhead.

Ben wasn't a bad guy—I would know—but he was about as war savvy as *America's Next Top Model*. And though I'd heard him more than once boasting about confirmed kills during his time in the field, he'd never once taken a human life. That was something else my gift could tell me. Death, murder or not, left marks like a tally on the mortal soul—and I could count them.

Lucky for Calvin, insecurity and being a douche doesn't automatically qualify someone for damnation—however unfortunate that may feel from time to time. But it sure as hell didn't help any of us in a combat situation under his command.

To make our bad position even worse, it was time for him to advance, and advancement tended to make officers batshit crazy. Especially those like Calvin who were riding the line between making rank or getting booted from the Corps.

He was using us to gain some attention and commendations to fill his advancement packet. Unfortunately for him, and thereby all of us, no one was watching. But Calvin was determined to do everything possible to turn heads in our direction. Even if that included the enemy's.

That was part of the reason we were rolling through the desert in noisy Humvees instead of leveling the IJS's shit with an airstrike. Hammerhead *said* it was because we needed visual proof that the weapons cache existed. And that *may* have been true to some extent, but we all knew he was itching for a high-profile showdown with the IJS.

The Recon motto, "Swift, Silent, Deadly," had no place on this mission, and I prayed it wouldn't get us killed. We'd been in the desert for less than a month, and we'd come close to losing men a few times already.

"What do we do?" Burch asked, looking at me.

I waved my finger forward. "Ask me again in a few minutes."

"Roger that."

In the back seat, Jim Wyatt (we called him "Earp") chuckled. "You know, I hate that we say 'roger that' to everything."

"Why?" Lance Corporal Nick Chavez, the new kid, asked.

"Because every damn time, Roger Rabbit pops into my head, and Roger

Rabbit makes me think of Jessica Rabbit, and then I can't think about anything other than my desperate, lonely cock."

"Thanks a lot, Earp. Now that's what we're *all* going to be thinking from here on out," I said, shaking my head.

Earp smiled. "You're welcome."

We all laughed.

My radio beeped. "Punisher, this is Chuckwagon. We've got a flat. Over."

I spoke into my microphone. "Can we push through? Not the best place to make a pit stop."

"Negative, Punisher. We've been riding on the rim for a while."

I swore. "We've got to stop. The supply truck's only got three legs."

A symphony of swearing chimed around the vehicle as I called in the need to stop to our command. A flat tire in the middle of hostile territory could be deadly. It might mean an ambush. More likely, it was proof of our dispensability to the government, evidence of budget cuts at the expense of our safety. While the latter reason was immediately more favorable, it was still a kick to the balls to those of us on the front lines of the War on Terror.

My senses were on high alert as the Humvee stopped. The shoddy landscape was shrouded in a ghostly green glow as I scouted for danger.

"Tabor, how's it looking?" I called up to the machine gunner, who was scouting the area with his Browning M2HB, the .50 caliber gun mounted on the top of our vehicle.

"All clear as far as I can see, Sergeant."

We were outside the heart of the city, but in no way was it a desolate area. There were plenty of rundown buildings and structures to provide camouflage for insurgents.

I slowly panned the sides of the road. A two-story building to our left was particularly troubling. In the distance behind it appeared to be the dome roof of a mosque. Call me racist or whatever, but given our mission, I wasn't taking a chance that it was a place of peaceful worship and not a place of inflammatory extremism.

I also knew the building was occupied. It was part of the same sense that knew the dog's meal in the road wasn't human. There were bodies inside, and they were alive.

"We need to clear that." I turned in my seat to look at my guys in the back. "I'm going in on point. Chavez, you'll be my number two. Earp, behind him, and Burch, you round us out."

"You're going in first?" Burch asked.

"Yeah." I would have a better idea of what was on the other side of that door once we got closer to it.

They nodded, and I called it in to our captain, who was two cars behind us. "Mongoose, this is Punisher One. We need to clear that building if we're taking a break here. My team's got it if you guys can cover us."

"Roger that. We've got your six," someone replied.

Before I gripped my door handle, I took a moment to lock my gaze with each of my men. It wasn't to intimidate, but to reassure. They needed to know I saw them.

Nick Chavez, our newest recruit on his very first tour, was sweating, and I doubted it was just from the heat. Burch, the seasoned vet with four tours under his belt and a new baby at home, was squared away with his hand on the door. And Earp—the guy who'd volunteered to go back to Iraq in place of someone who wanted to stay at home—had his goofy grin cemented in place. They were my guys. My responsibility.

"Let's move," I said.

"Roger that," Chavez replied.

"And just like that, I have a hard-on," Earp said.

We laughed quietly as we got out of the Humvee.

There were now four vehicles in our convoy, including the supply truck that had blown a tire. It was sitting at an angle, its metal rim resting on the rock-hard dirt.

I was in the lead car at our command's instruction. My ability to "see" things and read people had become legendary during my time in Afghanistan, even more so than my marksmanship. Once again, I'd found notoriety in being a freak rather than for my accomplishments.

It sucked.

The doors to the second Humvee opened in sync with ours, and the guys from the other teams fanned out to create a 360-degree perimeter around the convoy. Chavez, Earp, and Burch fell in step behind me as we crossed the road with our weapons aimed and ready to fire.

It was only when we neared the building that I realized the front window was boarded up. Through the crack was the faintest sliver of light. I pointed it out to the guys. They squared up in a tight line behind me, Chavez's hand was on my shoulder. I signaled to them that we were moving in, and I tried the door handle. It was unlocked, so I pushed it open.

There was no one directly in front of me, but just to the right of my gun's barrel were four elderly Iraqi men dressed in robes and white turbans.

"Down! Down! Down!" I shouted, turning my weapon in their direction as I rushed into the room.

They appeared to be religious leaders, and with one glance over their wrinkled faces, I knew they were *innocents*—a judgment not automatically deemed by their job title. It was disturbing the number of wicked people I encountered in deeply religious circles, and my gift could absolutely see what such souls would like to stay hidden.

Still, I followed cautious procedure for my guys, who didn't know what I did; I couldn't risk them picking up bad habits from their freak-of-a-sergeant that might get them killed.

I panned right. Chavez went left. Burch and Earp pressed in behind him.

It was clear the old men had been through this before. Immediately, they began to painfully sink to their arthritic knees on the packed dirt floor. Their hands were empty and raised above their heads.

One of them looked at me and gasped, so startled that he toppled over onto his hip. I wanted to help him, but I couldn't in front of my men.

"Clear this way," Earp said behind me.

"Clear," Burch echoed.

I grabbed a zip tie off the back of Chavez's kit and secured the first man's hands. I moved around to do the same with the others.

"Who else is in this house? Is anyone upstairs?" I demanded as I zip-tied the second man.

They were all shaking their heads and babbling in Arabic.

Everyone was terrified, but none so much as the man who'd fallen over. He was visibly shaking as I neared him. I lowered my weapon and reached for his hands. He cowered back.

"I'm not going to hurt you," I said, shaking my head.

His back was against the wall, his arms covering his face. "Azrael, no!"

I blinked with surprise. I was used to being called "Ali Baba" by the locals when they feared I might hurt them. It was a name understood between the Iraqi's and the US military to mean "bad guy." To most people, no matter the country, that's what I seemed to be. But *Azrael* was new. I grabbed the man's hands and tied them together.

When they were all secured, I backed into the corner near the stairs, where I could still see the old men and the door. I dropped to a knee and raised my weapon, watching all points of the room. My other sense told me the rest of the house was empty, but protocol demanded the other rooms be checked. "You three, clear upstairs. Burch, you're on point."

"Roger that," he replied.

My eyes were fixed on the man who was now crying in a heap on the floor. He looked at me, and I noticed his eyes. One was brown, the other pale blue. He began sobbing. "Azrael, no. Azrael, no."

"Who's Azrael?" I asked. "Is he here? Is he in this house?"

"Azrael, no!"

The conversation was pointless.

"All clear up top!" Burch called a moment later.

I spoke into my radio. "Mongoose, this is Punisher One. Over."

"Punisher One, this is Mongoose Actual. Send your traffic." Mongoose Actual was *actually* our captain speaking. Had it been anyone else on his team, they wouldn't have added the "actual" to the identification.

We could never be 100 percent sure who was listening to our coms, so anonymity was essential.

"Mongoose, we have four nonhostiles inside. All secured."

"Roger that, Punisher One. Over."

"Mongoose, can you send in the Canary? I feel like making some music," I said.

My radio beeped. "Roger that, Punisher One. Canary inbound. Over."

They were sending in our translator.

My guys reentered the room behind me. "Chavez and Earp, cover the windows. Burch, watch the door. The terp's coming in."

A moment later, Ahmed "the Canary" Saleem ducked through the front door. He was in full multi-cam with a helmet and a tan rag covering his face to hide his identity from the civilians. In their world, working with the US military could have lethal consequences.

I motioned him over, and he dropped down to a knee beside me. "Yes, sir. How may I help you, sir?" he asked, jittery as always.

I pointed at the frightened man, who was still doing everything in his power to avoid eye-contact with me. "Ask him who Azrael is."

Ahmed's head tilted slightly. "Azrael is the Hebrew name for the Angel of Death, the spirit being who separates the human soul from the body."

I nearly fell over. "Ask him *where* Azrael is."

Ahmed spoke to the man in Arabic.

Wordlessly, the old man raised a bony finger and pointed it right at me.

TWO

My knee was frozen to the floor. Visibly shaking, the old man in the turban retreated back into the cocoon of his arms around his head.

"Would you like to know anything else, sir?" the translator asked.

It took a second for my brain to register that he'd asked me a question. I shook my head. "No. Thank you. Tell them we'll cut them loose soon."

There were other questions I should have asked while I had the opportunity.

Questions about insurgent activity in the area and threats to us that could be local, but my thoughts were otherwise occupied tallying up the events of my life and weighing them against the old man's accusation.

The first time I took a human life I was eight.

That was the first time I could remember, anyway. I suspected there was one before that, probably my mother, which would explain why I was dumped in a church lobby in Chicago when I was only hours old. My umbilical cord had been sloppily severed and was still oozing blood when I was found.

In all, I'd dispatched forty-two souls from the earth. Thirty-three with my rifle. One with my bare hands. And eight with a force I couldn't explain.

That was how the first death happened.

I was in foster care at the time, sharing the home with a girl named Alice. She was seven and couldn't pronounce the letter *S*. Coupled with her contagious giggles, I thought it was the cutest sound in the world. The other kids gave her hell about it, though. Maybe that's why she liked me. They were too afraid of me to pick on her when I was around.

I'd grown accustomed to being feared by everyone. It was part of the consequence of being…whatever I was. But Alice was different, the first and only true friend I'd ever had. She enjoyed my company, a curiosity that both thrilled and unnerved me because, through her, I would learn the pain that could be born of caring.

The first few weeks of any placement were always the same. We were the adorable new pets, doted upon by the saviors of discarded children. Some foster parents would buy us new toys and clothes; others would simply be overly attentive and caring. But the novelty always faded, more quickly with me than with the others.

The inaugural week with Ellen Burke, an unmarried registered nurse at the local hospital, was no different. We moved into her house just after the first of the year, and she hosted a late Christmas for us, correctly assuming that our holiday celebration had been dismal. Our rooms were cozy and adequately stocked, adjacent to each other off of a short hallway upstairs.

We shared a wall, through which we developed our own version of Morse Code. Two knocks meant good morning or good night depending on the time of day. A staccato and rhythmic *knock. knock. knock-knock. knock. knock! knock!* meant "Do you want to play?"

For the first time I could remember in my short life, I was at peace with the world around me. I had a comfy bed, a decent school, and my very best friend—my only friend—just a knock on the wall away.

And in one day, that peace was ripped out from under me like a collapsing trapdoor.

The laws of the land were strict when it came to the government allowing people to foster kids. They went through rigorous screenings and background checks. They were subject to interviews and home studies.

It must have been for the sake of convenience that Ellen Burke's boyfriend moved out during her approval process to become a foster parent. I never thought she did it out of malice because, aside from her shitty taste in men, she was a good person.

Charlie Lockett was quite the opposite.

The moment he pulled into the driveway, my head began to swirl. Evil has an effect much like motion sickness. It can't be seen or touched, only felt—and I felt the evil inside him through the brick wall of the house. I puked my SpaghettiOs all over the shag carpet when he walked in.

The first month, nothing happened. Had my instincts not been the only thing in the world to never fail me, I might have thought I was wrong about Charlie. He was kind and caring, focusing on Alice most of the time. He showered her with praise and affection, patting her back and stroking her hair.

But before long, Alice started to change.

Her gaze stayed fixed on the ground most of the time. There was no more giggling. She stopped answering when I knocked on the wall. Every day, she retreated further and further into herself.

I didn't know what was happening. I was only eight. But I knew I was losing my friend, and I knew Charlie Lockett was responsible.

One day after school, Alice began crying as soon as we walked into the house. Charlie was waiting for us...waiting for her.

I stepped in front of her when he stood up from his recliner, my fists clenched in tiny balls at my side.

His head pulled back in surprise, and he laughed. "What is this?"

Angry tears spilled down my cheeks. I was shaking. "No more," I said through a clenched jaw.

His expression twisted from humored to hateful. That was when he lunged to grab me, and I threw my hand forward. A loud crack with the force of lightning reverberated around the room. The glass in the curio cabinet shattered. And Charlie Lockett fell forward, face-planting on the carpet near the same spot I'd vomited the first day we met.

It was over.

I told the social worker who came to get us that it was my fault Charlie died. She didn't believe me, of course. But it was true.

At eight years old, I was the judge, jury, and executioner.

Maybe the old man in the turban was right.

Maybe I was Azrael.

The Angel of Death.

Captain Mac Headley—call sign Mongoose—approached my vehicle when I walked back out to the road. Chaz started in our direction, but Headley held up a hand to stop him. Chaz's shoulders dropped. He was insulted to be left out of the conversation.

Next to Headley, I felt small. A strange feeling since I was 6'2 and pushing 225 pounds. I had to look up at him. "Yes, Captain?"

"The tire is changed on the supply truck. Everyone is riding ragged. What are your thoughts about stopping?"

"Hammerhead says——"

He held up a hand to silence me. "I know what Hammerhead says. I want to know what you think."

And that was the reason we all respected the captain. He listened. He'd started his military career as a grunt like the rest of us, was honorably discharged after completing his enlisted service, then finished his degree and returned to the Marines as an officer. He didn't have to be here. He could have stayed back on base with the rest of command and sent someone else. But he didn't. He was with his men.

I looked all around us and lowered my voice. "I'm not happy about the idea of stopping around here, but we need to get off the road and let the guys get some shut-eye." I looked up the road in front of us. "I say we stop at the designated spot and rest for a few hours."

He nodded and wordlessly slapped the back of my shoulder before walking in the direction of the second Humvee.

I climbed in my passenger-side door.

Burch looked over. "What's the plan, boss?"

I drummed my fingers on the armored plate of the door. "We stop as scheduled."

"Roger that," he said and put the transmission in gear.

"Roger that," Earp parroted back with a chuckle.

It made me smile.

Our scheduled stop for rest and rehydration was a supposedly abandoned building northeast of where the convoy had blown a tire. It was a short detour off the main road, over a sand berm, and behind what used to be a concrete wall that now lay in ruins. Inside the crumbling wall was the rubble of an old village that had probably been demolished by allied bombs during the 2003 invasion.

The sun was cresting over the horizon when we pulled to a stop in front of the only building still mostly standing. It was a two-story structure with the top-right corner blown out. Probably by an RPG.

I removed my night-vision goggles. My

eyes scanned the area while my other sense searched the atmosphere.

"If the hajjis don't kill us, the collapse of that building might," Earp said, looking out his window.

I didn't like being on the road, but I didn't like the thought of stopping here either. Our sister company had said the building was abandoned, but my gut said otherwise. An odd sensation radiated off its walls, and I knew we needed to push farther out of the city.

I pulled the microphone of my radio closer to my mouth. "Mongoose, this is Punisher One requesting permission to find a different hotel. Over."

"Standby," someone replied.

A moment later, the radio beeped. "This is Mongoose Actual. Request to find a different hotel has been denied. There are no more hotels on the map. We are to set a perimeter, secure the location, and get out of the heat. Over."

I groaned.

There was no way to get to a better

position without catching a rash of shit from command. And we'd have to inform them if we moved. The last thing we wanted was for our battlefield massacre to be labeled as a "training accident" because Hammerhead decided to prove himself by dropping an ass-ton of bombs on where he thought we weren't.

"Parish, what do you want to do?" Burch asked.

"Let's go to work and pray the LT back at base didn't flunk math at the Citadel."

They laughed. I didn't. I made a call over the radio. "Mongoose, this is Punisher One. We're going to check out the accommodations. Over."

"Roger that. Over."

My team formed up again to check out what was inside the concrete structure. I prayed it was as harmless as a creepy old guy in a turban. I doubted we'd get so lucky twice in an hour. Luck was not the way of war. And I already knew something sinister lurked inside.

With my gun pressed against my

shoulder and ready to fire, I pushed the front door open. What I saw stopped my feet dead in their tracks.

A woman.

An American woman.

THREE

The barrel of a Remington 700 tactical sniper rifle was pointed at my face. I was so startled by the dizzying eyes staring down it that it probably saved her life—or hell, it probably saved mine.

I blinked realizing it was a popular night for mismatched eyes. One of hers was dark chocolate, the other emerald.

There were more people in the room. I watched in my periphery as they all lowered their weapons slowly to the ground. The woman didn't. She kept her gaze and her sights set on me.

"Who the hell are you?" I demanded.

"Who the hell are you?" she fired back.

She wore tan camo fatigue pants, black boots, and a black sports bra. Her olive skin was tanned from the Iraqi sun, and her long dark hair was pulled up in a knot on top of her head. Even from the length of my weapon and hers, I smelled her, the scent of a woman so dangerously out of place in the desert.

One of the men to my right took a step toward me. Burch moved in fast with his rifle. "Hold up!" the man yelled. "Let's all take this down a few degrees so no one gets shot."

"Who are you?" I asked him.

"Contractors from Claymore. They call me Enzo." He held up an ID badge.

Burch stepped forward to inspect it, but I took an alarmed step back. Enzo's eyes— one green, one blue.

What the hell?

Aliens. Fucking aliens would be my luck. But that's not a question a man in uniform can ask without having his weapon confiscated by the team doc.

"Retired First Battalion, Fourth Marines, Bravo Company," Enzo added for good measure.

Claymore Worldwide Securities was one of the largest private militaries contracted to help us in the Middle East. Unbound by standard rules of engagement and the Geneva Convention, they could accomplish things we could only daydream about in the field. They also made a lot more money than we did, had better equipment, and got more time off.

We weren't exactly friends.

"Fury, lower your weapon," Enzo said.

The woman stared at me for a moment, then reluctantly lowered her gun, and I slowly lowered mine.

"Why didn't we know you were in the area? Are your transponders turned off?" I asked.

Enzo was smiling. "Nope. Broadcasting loud and clear."

My confidence in command was

officially in the toilet.

"What are you doing here?" Burch asked, returning Enzo's ID badge.

Enzo tucked the wallet back into the armored kit strapped to his chest. "Same as you. Liberating the world, one ungrateful Iraqi asshole at a time." He nodded toward the corner where a man in plaid shorts and a white shirt was handcuffed to his own ankles. A pillowcase was over his head. He was the source of all my bad feelings about the place, and seeing him restrained calmed my buzzing nerves.

"What is he wearing?" Burch asked.

Enzo smiled. "Golf shorts and a polo. Funny shit, right?"

Earp was laughing quietly behind me.

"We're taking him to Abu Ghraib. We stopped here to rest for a few hours, but we're on our way out," Enzo said.

I pressed the button on my radio. "Mongoose, this is Punisher One. You're not going to believe who we found in here."

"Punisher One, this is Mongoose Actual. I'm listening."

"Claymore contractors doing a transport. Over."

Earp stepped up beside me and shielded his mouth with his hand. "Tell them I'm calling dibs on Miss Tactical Titties."

Before any of us could react, the woman flipped her rifle around and slammed its stock into Earp's nose. He crumpled forward and fell to his knees. I instinctively raised my barrel at her face again, stunned but amused.

I nudged Earp with my boot. "You all right?"

"Not the first time a chick has done that," he replied, getting back to his feet. Blood poured into his mouth and dripped from his chin.

"Why doesn't that surprise me?" I lowered my weapon. The bridge of his nose was caved in and twisted sideways. I winced just looking at it. "That shit's broken. Go see Doc."

He started to turn.

"Earp!" I yelled.

"Yeah?"

"Apologize first."

"Sorry, ma'am," he said, using his scarf to catch the blood.

Her eyes narrowed.

God, she was hot, and I didn't have to be a mind reader to know everyone in the room was thinking the same. But no one else said it out loud, thanks to Earp. I wondered how many guys in her own unit she'd had to teach the same lesson. The way they moved out of her way as she crossed the room told me she'd earned their respect. She carefully placed her rifle into its case and turned back to look at me before I realized I was still staring.

I needed out of that room. Fast.

"When are you leaving?" I asked Enzo.

"As soon as we're packed up. I want to make Abu Ghraib before lunch so we can get to Camp Victory by this evening."

I raised an eyebrow. Victory was where my command was camped out, all the way across Baghdad. "Good luck. Lots of hot zones between here and there."

"We'll manage."

"On foot?"

His mouth bent into a small, mocking smile. "Of course not. Aren't you boys Recon?"

I considered punching him in the face.

"We'll wait for you to set an overwatch before we head out. More eyes on those hills, the better."

I gave a slight nod of agreement and turned to walk outside.

Headley was standing by his vehicle. "What's the status in there?"

"They're rolling out."

He nodded. "Is this a good place to make camp for a while?"

I looked around us. The rising sun was casting a golden hue over the rough terrain. "I still don't like it, but it will do for the next few hours. My team can take first watch."

"Since you've already got Chaz, take team three as well. I'll let him know. We'll relieve you in a few hours."

"How long do you expect us to be here?"

"We're supposed to roll out at fourteen-hundred hours, so we can make Tuz Sehir by nightfall."

"That's what we said *last* nightfall," I said with a grin.

He chuckled. "I know. Gotta love it when a two-day mission starts looking more like a week. Fucking IJS."

"Agreed." I panned the area again, this time looking for the highest point on the landscape. There was a large, rocky ridge a hundred yards behind the building that would give me a clear view of our surroundings. I pointed to it. "Burch and I will set up on that ridge. Once we've got the all clear, I'm going to let him get some sleep."

"Sleep in shifts. You need some rest too, Parish," he said.

I nodded, but I knew sleep probably wouldn't happen.

"McKenna!" Captain shouted, waving him over.

I walked back to my vehicle, where my guys were waiting for instruction. When the captain finished talking to McKenna, I called out to him. "Chaz, bring your team over here!"

He stared at me for a moment, like he was debating ignoring me or not. Then he signaled to his men, and the five of them walked over.

When they were close enough to hear, I looked at my guys. "Chavez and Tabor, you two will be taking first watch on patrol with team three."

Chavez groaned. "I'm so tired."

Newbie, indeed. "You'll have to be tired for a few more hours. Then you can rest. Earp will join you when he's finished with Doc."

"Since we don't have a vehicle, we'll take yours and vehicle two. We'll set them up on the east and west sides of the building." Chaz pointed, in case any of us were directionally challenged. "Tabor can man your fifty. Fradera can man the other."

Fradera, another corporal I didn't know too well, nodded.

"Where do you want me?" Chavez asked.

I answered, "with Tabor," at the same

time Chaz answered, "with Fradera."

I scowled at Chaz. "I can handle my team, McKenna. Thank you."

He bowed his head slightly but didn't speak.

"Chavez, you stay and watch Tabor's back until Earp is finished with the doc. Then Earp's your battle buddy. You stay with him."

"Roger that, Sergeant," Chavez said.

"Me and you?" Burch asked me.

"We'll be on the ridge."

"Roger that."

Burch had been my spotter since our tour in Afghanistan. He'd seen me do some strange things, including use my power to kill three members of Al-Qaeda who were walking the streets of Kabul wearing suicide vests. I'd had no other choice. Burch didn't ask questions though, and for that, I was thankful. He'd simply slapped me on the back and expressed his gratitude that I was on their side and not the enemy's.

At the top of the hill, I set up my rifle on its bipod, then stretched out on my stomach behind it. Through the scope I had a good view of the back of the building, the two Humvees on guard on either side of it, and the Marines in their watch positions around it. I saw Tabor in our turret and Chavez, holding a pair of binoculars, by the vehicle.

Tucked behind the ruins of an old block wall, two black SUVs were covered in desert-camouflage netting. I assumed they belonged to Claymore.

"Are you looking for her?" Burch asked as he settled in the dirt beside me.

"What?"

"That chick. Daaaa-yum."

I smiled. "No, I'm not."

"Well, move over and I'll look for her."

"You're married, dude."

He laughed. "My wife would understand. Jesus. What the hell is a woman like that doing in a shithole like this?"

I'd wondered the same thing. "Judging from Earp's broken nose, she could probably handle the IJS better than any of us."

"Hell yeah. That was hysterical. Fucking Earp."

One of Claymore's contractors pulled the netting off the SUV, and even though I truly wasn't looking for her, I did watch the woman walk all the way from the building to the vehicle. She wore a black tactical kit over her tank top, a handgun holster strapped to her thigh, and a 5.56 on a sling resting over her breasts. It was the sexiest sight I'd ever seen.

She got in the front-passenger's seat as Enzo guided their handcuffed and hooded Iraqi into the back seat behind her. Enzo got in, and before the door slammed shut, the SUV was rolling toward the road. "They're heading out."

Burch sighed. "Too bad. A view like that could make this whole war worth it."

I smiled. "Get some sleep. I'll take first watch."

"Parish, do you ever sleep?"

"Rarely."

"You're such a freak, man."

"I know."

It was almost full daylight outside, making it much easier to observe the area through my lens. The Claymore vehicle drove around the front of the building, then turned down the dirt road and disappeared from my view. The rest of our unit, those not on watch, went inside the building.

Aside from the faint *pops* of gunfire and mortars to the south, the village was quiet in those early hours. My shoulders relaxed behind my gun, and as I scanned the dry landscape, my brain rewound to the moment I pushed open that door and saw those eyes. Those curves. That smooth, taut skin.

Who was she?

The rapid fire from an AK-47 jolted me from my daydream. I scanned the area and saw nothing out of place. Marines in front of the building ran for cover behind the Humvees and began shooting in the direction of the road that ran alongside the village. Burch bolted upright, swearing as he straightened his armored helmet on his head.

"What happened?" he asked.

I thrust a pair of binoculars toward him. "I don't know. Can't see where the shots are coming from. Somewhere on the other side of that row of destroyed buildings."

"I can't see shit!" he yelled.

I clicked the button on my radio. "Mongoose, this is Punisher One. I've got zero visibility on the show up here. I need to move to find better positioning. Over."

Mongoose's response came quickly. "Move your ass, Punisher One. We need you. All targets declared hostile. Fire at will."

Burch and I grabbed our gear and ran east, just behind the ridge of the hill. He stumbled once on the loose rocks but recovered quickly and kept pace with me. We crested another peak and could finally see beyond the obstructing buildings through a wide gap likely left by the missile that had leveled the village.

We dropped to the ground. Men on foot and in trucks were firing on us from a tree line beyond the wall. I quickly estimated about forty targets, mostly armed with AKs.

I scanned back to the right. My Marines were now hidden by the building. I could only see Chaz's team and the Humvee that Fradera was firing the .50 Cal from.

When I panned left again, my eyes landed on a pair of men setting up an RPG tube.

I called in over the radio. "Mongoose, this is Punisher One. I've lost visual contact with you, but I've got two targets at our three o'clock at seven hundred meters who appear to be setting up an RPG tube."

"Punisher One, this is Mongoose Actual. You are approved to engage those targets. Over."

"Roger that."

I looked at Burch. "All targets hostile."

He gave a slight nod. Once again, I settled my rifle's stand in the dirt. Looking through the scope, I found the targets in my sights. Tunnel vision immediately settled in, but I knew Burch was beside me calculating my distance and conditions with his binoculars.

He spoke loud enough for me to hear. "Range to target, seven three niner. Wind moving east to west, half wind value."

I adjusted the knobs on my scope to account for the distance and wind, then I centered the crosshairs on the head of the man holding the tube. "On target."

"Fire," Burch said softly.

I pulled the trigger. A half a beat later, I

watched the man's head explode and his body fall back and sideways.

"Stand by for second target," Burch said.

I put my sights on the other man, who was panicking and turning to run. "I got him."

"Fire."

The second bullet caught the second man somewhere in the ribcage, no doubt blowing a hole through his chest cavity that would kill him quickly.

"Hit," Burch said, patting me on the shoulder.

Then just as I looked up from the scope

—

POW!

The blast from another rifle startled both of us. Burch ducked, but I looked over in time to see a man's turban get blasted from his head. He tumbled down the hill face-first, his feet flying up over his lifeless body.

At the bottom of the hill was the woman they called Fury. Smoke was still rising from the end of her barrel as she took another shot toward a second man hiding in the bushes. His body lurched sideways and rolled down the rocky terrain. We hadn't even noticed them flanking us less than a hundred yards away.

She caught my eye and flashed a mocking smile. Then she ducked behind a piece of the old wall and disappeared from view.

Burch grabbed my sleeve. "What the hell was that?"

"That was us having our asses saved by a civilian. Come on. Our team is still under fire."

The enemy was closing in on the building. They were going to overtake it soon. Someone was yelling for them to get to higher ground over the radio, which meant they were coming to me.

Burch and I low-crawled back across the ridge and moved behind a cluster of rock formations down the face of the hill. Once we were settled, I had a decent view of the action below.

I looked through my scope again. "I've got two targets with AKs in range."

"All targets are declared hostile," Burch reminded me as he looked through his binoculars.

I nodded and chambered a round. He

called out the distance and wind, and I adjusted my scope accordingly. I breathed in and held it.

"Fire."

I pulled the trigger and watched the man fall backward. I reset and aimed at the other man.

"Fire."

He fell out of sight behind the tailgate of the truck.

Boom!

Kaboom!

It was the unmistakable strike of an RPG. There must have been a second team we'd missed. Beyond the berm and around the other side of the wall, a large puff of white smoke rose into the air.

I swore. "That had better not be another one of our vehicles."

Bursts of gunfire echoed all around us. Burch and I took out another shooter coming around the side of our building. Two groups of Marines launched grenades toward the incoming line of fire to give them time to make it up the ridge.

Boom! Boom!

When the smoke and dust cleared, the

enemy militants were scrambling, including the second RPG team. Well, one of them was scrambling; the other was dead. The survivor laid down behind a broken slab of concrete and pulled the RPG tube across the dirt toward him.

I set the sites of my rifle on his body. Burch called out the position. I adjusted. Breathed.

"Fire."

Nothing happened.

"Fuck."

"What is it?" Burch asked.

"Jammed."

I looked through my scope again. The RPG was loaded into the tube. The tube was seated on the operator's shoulder, and his finger was on the trigger.

"Burch, three o'clock."

The second Burch turned his head, I extended my hand and released my energy across the battlefield. The thunderous jolt through the heavens would be easily mistaken for a grenade or a mortar.

Immediately, the man's body was blasted backward behind a pile of rocks. His feet, the only thing still visible, didn't even twitch.

I was lowering my hand when Burch's face whipped back toward me. "Three o'clock?" he shouted angrily as he brought his scope up and looked toward the RPG team again. His mouth fell open when he looked at me.

I shook my head slowly, warning him not to ask questions.

The Marines, now scattered along the ridge around us, showered the enemy below with gunfire and more explosives.

After ten or a hundred minutes—I couldn't tell—Mongoose began yelling, "Cease fire!" over the coms. The gunfire waned to silence.

The enemy was gone. Or dead, with any luck.

I searched the horizon and saw their remaining trucks throwing up dirt and dust behind them as they retreated south and out of sight.

No one moved until we were sure the threat was over. Then, finally, I pushed myself up off the ground. "Come on, Burch. Let's go check on the guys."

My hearing slowly returned, though everything still sounded hollow and far away.

THE MERCENARY

Someone was screaming down below us.

FOUR

Lance Corporal James "Cinnamon" Spicer, a twenty-two-year-old farm boy from Iowa, had taken a round to the collar bone while calling out the position of an Iraqi gunner. The bullet had missed his artery by less than three inches.

It hadn't taken long once I started my military career to figure out that sick or injured people got worse around me, so I kept my distance as they took him back inside the cleared building.

When we found him, Tabor was back inside the turret, trying to dislodge a jammed round from the .50 Cal. "Wes, where's Chavez?" I called up to him.

Tabor shrugged. "With Earp, I think."

"Come on," I said to Burch.

We walked inside and looked around at the Marines starting to defuse from the adrenaline rush. Some were sitting. A couple were sprawled on the floor. Some were cleaning their weapons. Others were smoking cigarettes. All of them were wide eyed and still panting.

Earp was laughing with a gunner from team three.

I grabbed the collar of his shirt and spun him around. His nose was covered in a wide white bandage, and bloody gauze was shoved up his nostrils. His eyes would be black before too long.

Burch cringed. "Geez, dude. That shit looks awful."

"Doc was in the middle of resetting it when those hajjis lit us the fuck up."

"Where's Chavez?" I asked.

He blinked. "Haven't seen him since before shit went down. He's probably with Tabor."

"We just saw Tabor. He thought Chavez was with you," Burch said.

Dread was pooling in my stomach like battery acid as I searched the room again.

"What the hell happened out there?" Enzo stalked through the front door of the building right behind me. "This has been a relatively peaceful mission until the goddamn Marines show up."

Burch took a step toward him, and my hand slammed against his chest plate to hold him back. "We might have said the same thing about Claymore," he said and spat over my arm at Enzo's feet. "They weren't here looking for us!"

Enzo stuck his finger in Burch's face.

"You might want to start counting your lucky stars Claymore was here to save your ass. If it weren't for Fury, you'd be going home in a cardboard box, Sergeant."

He had a point.

"We lost our prisoner. They took him." Enzo put his hands on his hips. "And one of our SUVs was hit by an RPG."

"Was anyone inside?" Headley asked.

Enzo shook his head. "No, but now we're down a vehicle and missing a hostile target."

"We're dealing with our own shit here, Enzo." Headley motioned around the room full of chaos. "You're on your own."

"Not if we're after the same enemy, Captain. And there's only one around this area."

Enzo was right. The IJS was the only organized group still at large on this side of Baghdad. With that big of a militia *and* the fact that they'd freed Claymore's target, chances were undeniable we were after the same mark.

Headley jerked his head toward the door. "Warren, take your guys to see who's dead. And find out which way the survivors were headed."

"Captain, we have another problem. I'm missing one of my guys."

"Who?" Headley asked.

"Lance Corporal Nick Chavez, sir."

"Everybody, listen up!" Headley shouted, his booming voice instantly silencing the room. "We're looking for Nick Chavez. Anybody seen him?"

One of the Marines on team three raised his hand. "Sergeant McKenna sent him with me and Morley up to the second floor to return fire."

Chaz was standing behind him.

I started toward him. Then it was Burch's turn to stop me. "You did what?"

"We were getting hammered out there! We needed eyes up above returning fire over that wall, so I sent him with Morley and

Finn," Chaz said.

"I told you not to give my men orders! Where the fuck is he?"

Chaz stammered. He didn't have an answer.

"When the call was made for us to move to the ridge, me and Morley went down the stairs in the back, but Chavez went down the front staircase, the way we'd come in," Finn said.

I looked at Burch and lowered my voice. "He went back to find Earp and Tabor."

"Most likely, sir."

A heavy hand came down on my shoulder. It was Headley. "We'll find him. Go check those bodies and see which way they went."

"Roger that. Earp! Let's go." Burch and Earp followed me out of the building. "Tabor, you got that gun working?" I shouted up to him.

"Yes, sir!"

"Good. Get your ass down and come help us. We need to find Chavez."

Tabor caught up with us as I counted the bodies that had fallen at the village wall. "Only three here," I said, looking at the rubble.

We picked our way through the broken concrete and crossed the dirt road on the other side. Then we went down a hill and started across the field toward the trees.

Quick movement on the rocks behind us made us all turn and raise our weapons.

Fury and another man—stocky with a shock of red hair—descended the hill, dust kicking up around their boots as their footing slid on the slope.

I lowered my rifle. "What are you doing?"

"Watching your six," Fury said with a sneer. "God knows you'll probably need it."

Earp leaned toward me. "She's hot, but can I please shoot her?"

"Want some missing teeth to go with that nose?" the man asked, his finger on the side of the gun's trigger that was strapped across his chest.

"Who are you?" Burch asked.

The man lowered his voice to a growl. "Your worst nightmare."

We all laughed.

Fury rolled her eyes. "His name's Huffman. Lead the way. We're following whether you like it or not."

"Come on," I said to Earp and turned back toward the front wall.

Death was sprinkled along the tree line in the distance. I felt it as clearly as I felt the morning sun on my face. Fresh death was so much easier to detect. I counted the corpses without even seeing them. Six in the brush. Four scattered near the ridge where they'd flanked us.

I pointed that direction. "Earp, you and Tabor go check the base of the ridge for bodies."

"Roger that, sir," Earp replied.

The two of them turned left and headed toward where Burch and I had nearly been ambushed. "Thanks for saving us back there," I said to Fury.

Her head slightly tipped up to acknowledge the gratitude, but she didn't comment. Surprising since I expected more shit from her about it.

"How long have you all been in the field?" Huffman asked, falling into step with me as we walked toward the brush.

"Few days. You?"

"Same."

"Where'd you pick up your target?"

"A compound outside Tuz Sehir."

Yep. Same bad guys we were after. "That's where we're headed."

"Looks like that's where we're all headed," Huffman said.

Fury was walking the wrong direction.

"Bodies are this way!" I called out.

She stopped, her boots churning against the rocks in the dirt as she turned.

Burch looked over with a raised eyebrow. "How the hell do you know that? I don't see anything."

Shit.

I pointed across the rocky terrain to where I knew a body was concealed by the bushes. "You don't see that boot?" I lied. God, I hoped there was a boot.

He narrowed his eyes and said nothing.

Recent death left waves in the atmosphere, sort of like heat rising off fresh asphalt on a hot summer day. It rippled the air surrounding the corpses and pulled at my attention like a magnet.

When we reached them, there were six, like I already knew. "We shall call you Eagle Eyes," Burch said, patting the back of my shoulder. "Good work, Parish."

"All I did was count, man." I looked over

the bodies again, searching for a uniform like mine. "Our guy isn't here."

"That's a good thing, bro," Huffman said as we walked back toward the village.

There were fresh tire tracks that veered off the road and through the open desert in the direction I'd seen them go.

Fury walked over and stood beside me.

"What are you thinking?" I asked her.

She shielded her face from the sun as she looked out over the desert. "I think we just got lucky as hell. We can follow those tire tracks for a while. At least until they get to a main road."

That was exactly what I was thinking.

She continued. "My guess is they'll turn north at some point and head straight back to the hole where we found them, hoping to fortify the grounds—"

"And blow us all to hell with the explosives they've got stocked there," I added.

She nodded. "That's what I would do."

"You scare me, woman," Huffman said.

"Good." She was smiling as she touched the discreet microphone hidden in her ear. "I think we're going back to the hornet's nest, boys. Body count...?" She looked at me.

"Nine," Burch answered.

"Thirteen," I corrected.

Burch was looking at me like I was a freak again, but I grinned and pointed to where Earp was near the road holding up four fingers.

Burch and Huffman laughed.

"Thirteen," Fury said.

I clicked on my radio. "Mongoose, this is Punisher One. Over."

"Punisher One, this is Mongoose Actual. Send your traffic."

"We've got thirteen confirmed dead and no other targets in sight. Enemy tracks lead east through the desert, possibly to head back to the main compound. Either way, they'll be easy to follow."

"Roger that. Head back this way, Sergeant. We've got news on your boy. Over."

"Good news, sir?"

No answer.

They found Chavez's rucksack in the front stairwell of the building. It was open and its contents had been strewn across the floor. His MREs were missing. So was his KA-BAR knife and his gun-cleaning kit.

Chavez was gone. The enemy had him.

I swore and threw the rucksack against the wall. Then I turned and charged Chaz, who was standing right behind me. "I'm going to kill you!"

Headley and Burch held me back. "This isn't helping," Burch said calmly in my ear.

"We'll find him," Headley added. "But you need to calm down."

With a painful huff, I stepped back, then turned and stormed outside. I paced the front roadway with my hands laced on top of my head. It felt like my brain was going to explode, racing in too many directions at once.

Headley called the situation into command, and miraculously, they approved for us to start immediately tracking the enemy. *Immediately*, however, was going to take a couple of hours. Team two's Humvee had taken a lot of fire. Luckily, the guys thought they could fix it.

In the meantime, there was nothing to do but wait. And the waiting was brutal. It was like I could hear every single second ticking by in my head.

Aside from the obvious reason time was precious, another downside to our delay was that every second we waited was more time for the enemy to prepare. They already knew we were coming for them. In fact, they may have planned for us to follow them, taking Chavez as bait to lead us to an IED field or another ambush.

The only upside was a few of us were able to get a little rest. Not me, of course, but no surprise there. And where we were was probably the safest place in all of Iraq. At least here, all our enemies were confirmed dead.

It didn't take long for Burch to pass out under the shade of our camo netting as soon as we were back in position. After a while, my prone position in the dirt started causing the muscles in my lower back to spasm. I sat up, and my dangling dog tags clinked against my breastbone as I sat back against my rucksack.

The sound of boots coming up the hill behind me made me turn.

Fury.

She was carrying the Remington, and I wasn't sure which was sexier: her or the weapon. That was, until she sat down in the dirt beside me, facing the opposite direction so I had a clear view of the sweat drizzling down her tan cleavage.

Good god.

My heart was pounding so hard I feared she might hear it. How long had it been since I'd been so close to a female? It was a rarity, for sure. Chicks were scarce in the desert, and back at home, all but an unusual few kept their distance from me.

It wasn't because I was a bad-looking guy. At 11 percent body fat, my six-pack alone was enough to turn a few heads in my direction. But the breakdown in attraction seemed to occur at somewhere around six to eight feet in any direction.

I'd seen it a thousand times. Girls eyeing me across the bar or the gym, finally working up the nerve to approach…then boom. Six to eight feet out, they turn and make a bee-line for the nearest exit.

It was like I was born with a force field.

Yet here was this woman, her elbow

nearly grazing my sleeve without so much as a flinch. Maybe she was a sadist who got off on danger and fear. Maybe she was a really good actress, secretly screaming on the inside. Or maybe her nerves were steeled by the fact that she'd killed almost as many people as me. Thirty-seven, unless I was wrong.

And my gift had never been wrong.

Whatever the reason, her presence was intoxicating, a much-needed distraction when all I had to do was watch and *think*.

"My command sent me to protect our interests," she said, checking the bolt on her rifle.

"That's insulting."

"We did just get ambushed." I could almost see her rolling her eyes behind her dark sunglasses.

"They stole your prisoner. I don't think they were after us," I reminded her.

She looked through her scope. "Fair

enough. Want to steal some shut-eye while I keep watch?"

"I'm good." I scanned the horizon beyond the building that housed my brothers, an effort to keep my focus where it should be instead of on the cavern that dipped behind the neckline of her tank top.

"You worried about your guy?" she asked.

I didn't answer.

She nodded, understanding I didn't want to talk about it.

We were quiet for a while, and I let my mind drift away from Chavez to maintain my sanity. That was easy with her sitting beside me. I tried to figure up how long it had been since I'd felt the warmth of the fairer sex.

A *while* is what I came up with.

I needed to think of anything besides her after that.

She finally looked over her shoulder at

me and broke the loaded silence. "So... come here often?"

I cracked a smile. "More often than I'd like. You?"

"Third time this year."

"You deploy that often with Claymore?"

"Yeah, but that's not the norm. I volunteered to come back," she said.

That was surprising. "Money that good?"

She laughed and nodded. "Bet your ass it is."

I chuckled.

"How long have you been over here?" she asked.

"This tour?"

"Yeah."

"Almost a month."

"That sucks. How much time do you have left in the Corps?"

I did the math quickly in my head. "A little less than two years if I don't re-sign."

She groaned. "Why would you re-sign? Get out, and if you still want to shoot shit, go private. With a Recon background, you'd get picked up without a problem."

"Is that what you did?"

"Hell no." She settled her rifle on its bipod. "I've been with Claymore my whole career."

My head snapped back. "What? Did you start as a receptionist and work your way up to a gunner?"

"What kind of sexist bullshit is that? Do I look like a fucking receptionist to you?"

No. She looked like a tactical sex kitten, but I was pretty sure saying so might get me shot.

I grinned. "No offense intended. That's just pretty rare, isn't it?"

She lowered her sunglasses to look over them at me. "*I'm* pretty rare."

"No argument here." I shifted in the dirt. "Can I ask you a personal question?"

"Maybe."

"Your eyes. They're different colors. That's pretty rare too."

"That's not a question, Sergeant."

"No, but you and your commander both have them."

She stared at me for a second. Probably trying to decide if she should laugh or back away slowly. "You mean Enzo?"

I nodded.

The corner of her mouth twitched. "Don't worry. It's not a hiring requirement."

Tension eased in my shoulders. "I thought it might be a coincidence."

More silence.

"We're not related if that's what you're asking."

I didn't know what I was asking. "I think I've only ever met one person in my life with different-colored eyes, and I've seen three of you in the past few hours."

"Three of us?" Her question carried a

tone that stoked the idea that she knew more than me...because she probably did. "Who else?" she asked.

My head tilted toward the road we'd come by. "Old man earlier today. He called me Azrael."

I was watching her to gauge her reaction. She didn't have one.

"The Angel of Death," she said.

"You speak Hebrew?"

She shrugged. "God, no. Everybody knows that though."

"Not everyone."

"Maybe not *you*."

I grinned.

"Kind of an appropriate nickname for a trigger man though, isn't it?" she asked.

I smirked. "Right."

"What's your team's plan for attacking the IJS compound?"

"I wouldn't tell you if I knew," I said with a laugh.

"Don't trust me, huh?"

"Hell no."

She leaned toward me and sent my blood pressure up toward the Iraqi sun. "Can I give you a bit of advice?"

"No."

She ignored me. "You shouldn't attack from the south because they know where you are. They'll be expecting it, and it's the way we already hit them when we captured their guy. Flank them, or travel around and come in from the north."

I tugged on the collar of my uniform where my rank was pinned. "See these stripes? These stripes mean this guy doesn't make those decisions."

"I've heard you talking to your captain. He listens to you."

I laughed sarcastically. "No, he doesn't."

"Well, if you go in from the south, we already drove through the chain-link fence, so you'll have that working for you."

"Good to know. How many fighters will we encounter?"

"Sixty. Maybe more. But maybe less if it was the same guys who ambushed us earlier. We also took out a few of them when we were there, but once we got our guy, we hauled ass out."

"Who was he?"

"Yazen al-Zawbai, director of general security and intelligence for the IJS."

My head snapped back. "Interesting timing to remove the head of security just when we're going in to take the whole place down. Who are you working for?"

She shrugged. "That information is way above my pay grade." A thin smile spread across her full lips as she watched the horizon. "Too bad you guys screwed that up for all of us."

"Right."

"I'm going to see if I can get a better visual on the remaining Claymore vehicle.

You think you can handle this spot on your own?" She pushed herself up and brushed off the seat of her cargo pants.

God, her ass was perfect.

"I'll do my best," I said as my distracted eyes darted back to the horizon.

She dropped the strap of her rifle across her chest and adjusted the radio in her ear. "I need you to do better than that, Warren. We can't afford to lose another SUV."

I almost laughed, but another thought stopped me. "Hey, how do you know my name?"

Her gaze fixed on me for a long moment. Her mouth parted as her brain seemed to scramble for an answer. Then she knelt, hooked her finger around the chain of my dog tags, and leaned dangerously close to my face. "It's on your chain, dumbass. You're not the only person up here staring at chests."

FIVE

It took two hours for the guys to get the Humvee running again, but once it was mobile, we were quickly loaded and ready to head back out.

Chaz didn't say another word to me even after we'd left the village. He was sitting in Chavez's empty seat, a fact that pissed me off even more. If it wouldn't have risked additional confusion, I would have insisted he switch vehicles with someone else.

Claymore followed us in their remaining

SUV.

We were all extra vigilant as we followed the tire tracks through the desert. The daylight helped *and* hurt us. Helped because it would be easier to spot IEDs. Hurt because the sun was a sweltering spotlight announcing our presence in enemy territory.

The tracks led west, then northwest, and finally almost directly north. We had traveled off-road about twenty klicks before ever seeing what looked to be a road off in the distance. There was nothing else around us as far as I could see.

When we reached the road, the tracks disappeared as they mixed in with the others, but not before they made a definite arch north.

Headley called over the radio to tell us to stop. He and team two's leader, Kyle Pearson, met me and Chaz when we stepped out of our vehicle. Headley was carrying his Plexiglas map board. He opened it and laid it across the hood of the Humvee.

"We're here, gentlemen." He pointed at a road. "Warren, I think you're right that they're taking him back to the compound."

Pearson shrugged. "Where we were headed anyway."

"I'm so glad this is convenient for you, Kyle," I snapped.

He put his hands up. "No disrespect intended, Parish."

Headley glared at me. "Focus, please." He turned back to the map. "In thirty klicks, we'll pass through the village of Baheth. I want to see what intel we can gather from the locals. I want to know who's come through their town today. If we're heading in the right direction, the IJS should have passed through there."

Chaz looked up. "You don't think we're too exposed without any backup?"

It was Headley's turn to snap. "We're looking for a missing Marine. We'll be our own backup."

"What about Claymore?" I asked, pointing behind our convoy.

Over Headley's shoulder, I saw Fury adjusting something on the front of our communications guy's uniform. He was smiling from ear to ear. She was laughing. I didn't like it. Nothing in me trusted that woman, no matter how good she looked in multi-cam fatigues.

"Claymore is not a part of our mission," Headley said.

Pearson laughed. "Anyone told them that?"

"We're under orders, gentlemen. We're the United States Marine Corps. We do not work with civilian contractors." Headley looked around at all of us. "Understood?"

"Roger that," we all said together.

"On the other side of Baheth is another fifty klicks to the city of An Zahab, population a hundred and fifteen thousand. It's the last large hub of civilization between us and our target. Our objective is to haul ass through it."

"No collecting intel?" Pearson asked.

"We'll have better luck getting the locals to talk in Baheth. We're not stopping in the city. Too big of a risk and we'll be losing daylight."

We all nodded.

"After that, it's an open forty klicks to the target. The compound is on the south side of Tuz Sehir, just inside the city. We should reach it by dusk. With what went down here today, we've lost the element of surprise, so I hope everyone is ready for this to get ugly."

"What's the plan when we reach the factory?" I asked.

"We're going to stay away from Tawuq Highway and drive north, and enter the compound from this service road to the south."

I stepped forward and put my finger on our position. "Maybe we should consider bypassing the big city altogether. We could take this road here to the west, go around An Zahab, come out here, and take this road into Tuz Sehir. That way, we could either hit them from the side or from the north, where they're not expecting it."

"Hammerhead wants us to come in from the south just after nightfall," Headley said.

Pearson leaned over for a closer look. "Warren's right, Captain. They'll expect us to come in here, but if we take this road to the northeast, this side street would give us a direct—"

With a huff, Headley stepped back and reached through my window of the Humvee and grabbed the field phone. He waved the receiver toward us. "Either of you want to phone this up to command?"

My shoulders dropped.

Pearson looked away. "No, sir."

"All right then." Headley slammed the phone back down and returned to the map. "We are to launch a full-frontal assault on the compound. Once the target is in sight, we'll have all weapons come inline side-by-side, and we'll push forward until we meet resistance. Then we'll open fire."

"What if they kill Chavez when we open fire?" I asked, because I was the only Marine in our group who would dare.

"They won't," Headley said. He looked me square in the eye and shook his head. "They won't."

I nodded, but said nothing.

He continued. "Once we penetrate the compound, our first objective is to locate and rescue Chavez. All targets are declared hostile. They've had plenty of time to surrender.

"When they're down and done, we'll send in a sweep team to check the area. When the area is verified as cleared, we'll plant the explosives, and lay enough C-4 so that all of Iraq will know we were there."

That made all of us smile.

"Any questions?" Headley asked.

"And what if they've laid bombs on the road Hammerhead wants us to take?" Pearson said, his tone tight with anger.

A muscle was working in Headley's jaw. "We stay vigilant, just like always."

"Anything else?"

I shook my head. "No, sir."

Headley folded the map board closed.

"OK. Mount up."

I got back in my vehicle and thumped my head against the back of the seat.

"That bad, huh?" Burch asked, still behind the wheel.

"Did you hear any of that?"

"That we're probably going to have our asses blown right off that dirt road? Nah, I didn't hear any of that."

"Shut up, Brayden."

"Did he say we're taking the compound after dark?"

"Yeah. Probably because night vision will look so much cooler on CNN."

He grinned over at me. "Not to mention how impressive the explosives are in the dark. Rocket's red glare, and all that."

I actually chuckled.

"You gonna be all right, Warren? You haven't slept at all."

"I'll be fine. Twenty-four hours ain't nothin'."

"Except that it's been more like thirty-six." He reached into the front pocket of his uniform and produced a black bottle half full of caffeine pills. "Here."

"Thanks." I unscrewed the cap, poured a few caplets into my mouth, and swallowed them without any water.

My radio beeped. "Punisher One, this is Mongoose. We're oscar mike," someone from the captain's vehicle said.

I closed my door with more force than necessary. "Mongoose says we're on the move, guys. Let's go."

Lunch consisted of an energy bar and water just before we rolled into Baheth. I'd almost forgotten what home-cooked food tasted like. Not that anyone ever cooked for me back at home, but I'd learned a lot from YouTube, and I enjoyed cooking for myself. In fact, the night I was called up for this particular mission, I'd mastered the perfect roasted pork loin with a port-wine glaze. It was damn good too.

Sadly, if this mission continued on its downward spiral of suck, I might never be able to stomach that delicious meal again.

Somewhere nearby in Baheth, someone was cooking lamb and onions. Beside me, as we walked down the semi-crowded street, Earp's stomach growled loud enough for me to hear.

"Have you had anything to eat?" I asked, my eyes everywhere but on him.

"Some jerky and a melted Reese's Cup. You?"

"A superfood, high-protein bar made with chia seeds, rolled oats, and organic quinoa."

He laughed. "You're such a fruitcake, man."

"I'm a fruitcake that will outlive you."

"You say that like we might actually make it back to base alive." He was laughing. Gallows humor at its best. "Speaking of dying, on a scale of one to I'm-going-to-hell, how wrong is it that I'm really happy to see all these motherfuckers out here roaming the streets today?"

"You're going to hell regardless, but you're not the only one thinking it." Foot traffic meant no pressure plates to detonate explosives in the dirt. When the locals disappeared, that was a sign for us to be worried.

I couldn't talk about dying anymore, so I changed the subject. "How's the schnoz?"

"Hurts like a bitch." He gave a singsong sigh over the rumble of Humvee rolling beside us. "But, god, it was worth it. I'd take the butt of that chick's rifle again any day."

"Keep that talk up and you might."

I glanced behind us. No one from Claymore was on foot. Of course, why would they be? There was no need for them to talk to the locals. They already knew what we needed to know. Too bad the Marine Corps doesn't play well with others. It would save the tread on my boots and the strain on my spine.

"Your face looks ridiculous by the way," I told him.

He turned toward me. "I'm a sexy beast, Parish."

A flash of red caught my eye, and I looked over at him. "Dude, your nose is pouring blood again." The white bandages on his face were soaked.

I wondered if I was causing it.

In a flurry of profanities, he pulled a rag from his back pocket and pressed it to his face.

"Get back in the Humvee and clean that —"

He nudged my shoulder, then nodded past me. "Yo. Six o'clock."

I turned as an old Iraqi approached us from a store on the side of the road. He wore a traditional ankle-length robe and a scarf on his head. He waved his hand to make us stop. I got no menacing vibes off the guy, but Earp stepped beside me and pulled his rifle closer to his chest.

The man was babbling in Arabic, none of which I understood.

Earp whistled over his shoulder toward the convoy. "Canary! We need you!"

Ahmed was walking with the captain. They both came over. Headley was scouting for danger as usual when his eyes landed on Earp. "Wyatt, go see Doc and get that shit taken care of."

"Roger that, sir."

Behind us, the convoy had stopped. Guns were pointed in a 360-degree perimeter.

Ahmed spoke to the man. They exchanged a lot of words very quickly.

"What's he saying?" Headley asked.

"He's wants to know if we're looking for the IJS," Ahmed said.

"Tell him yes. Did he see them come through here today?"

"He said they came through this morning."

"How many men?" I asked.

Ahmed asked the man. After he gave a longer answer than a single number, Ahmed translated. "They didn't stop today, but they had four or five vehicles. He says they come through here a lot. His family owns a restaurant close by, and a few of them eat there from time to time."

Probably on weapons runs to and from

Baghdad and Sadr City.

The old man continued. He pointed up the road ahead. Ahmed spoke. "They come from Tuz Sehir. It's their headquarters. He knows because his brother's house is on the same street."

I groaned at the reminder that the place we were headed was in a heavily residential area.

"He doesn't want any trouble here in his town. He says this is a peaceful village. Lots of families here. He doesn't want anyone to get hurt."

"Tell him neither do we," Headley said. "Ask him if he knows of the IJS planting any kinds of explosives anywhere. Do we have anything to worry about here?"

Ahmed asked and listened to the man's response. "He says this is a peaceful village. The IJS only eats here sometimes. And today, they did not stop."

The old man grabbed my forearm and spoke directly to me.

"He said"—Ahmed cleared his throat before he continued—"outside the village, death awaits."

SIX

We pushed through the village, never letting our guard down for a second no matter how peaceful the old man said the place was. As we neared the edge of town, and the landscape turned from buildings back to dirt and sand, the back of my neck prickled.

Death awaits.

"High alert, guys," I warned all the men in my vehicle. "You see something, anything at all, you speak up loud and clear."

The standard operating procedure for IED detection was anything but standard. After all, there was no surefire way to prevent your murder if some psycho was determined to kill you, right? But we had a list of things to look for: objects on the roadside, exposed wires, cinderblocks, dead animals—even dead humans.

Outside of town, our eyes searched for piles of dirt, potholes filled over, and cracks in the shoddy pavement. An IED could really be hidden anywhere.

"Incoming vehicle," Burch said.

My face whipped forward. "Stop the car."

Vehicle-borne IEDs were a whole different thing altogether, and the IJS was definitely not above letting their own die to take out a few of us. Command would have to make a very quick decision to roll the dice on a suicide bomber or blow up innocent civilians if they missed our signals to halt.

Unfortunately, my sixth sense knew the difference between the good guys and the bad—and command often didn't listen to me. And people wondered why I didn't sleep much.

I reached for my radio as Burch rolled to a stop. "Mongoose, this is Punisher One. We have a vehicle inbound." I strained my eyes. "Looks to be a large truck or SUV." It was too far for me to get a reading on who was inside it. "Should we fire warning shots?"

"Dear Marine Corps," a man's voice boomed over the radio. "That would be a Claymore vehicle. Please don't blow it up." The guy sounded like Huffman.

Burch and I looked at each other.

Headley's voice came over the radio. "Claymore, what are you doing on our frequency?"

"Lucky guess," the man answered.

"Fury gave Claymore our frequency channels," I said to my guys. "She was flirting with Leake right before we pulled out."

"That bitch is good." Earp laughed and shook his head.

"I don't think you should call her a bitch," Chaz said, the first words he'd uttered since we'd loaded up.

Earp reached over and knocked on his helmet. "Think I need a lesson in manners, Sarge?"

Chaz nodded. "I kinda do."

"Might as well save your breath, McKenna. That's a losing war right there," Burch said.

The radio beeped again. "Kane, flash your lights so the Marines don't fire an RPG into your grill," Huffman said.

The SUV speeding toward us flashed its lights. I relaxed a little. In my rearview mirror, I saw the passenger-side door of the third Humvee fly open and Headley angle out of it. He stormed back past the supply truck to Claymore's vehicle and went out of my view when he crossed over to the driver's side.

"Somebody's getting an ass chewing," I

said.

Burch was watching in his mirror too. "I really want to go back there and watch."

Claymore's other black SUV, one that was noticeably cleaner and showing zero field damage, slowed as it passed by us. Its windows were completely opaque, hiding whoever was inside. A strange energy seemed to hum around it, and I suddenly felt like a planet passing too close to a black hole.

It was unlike anything I'd ever felt before.

"Warren?" Burch's voice startled me.

"Huh?"

"I said, at least we know the road ahead is somewhat clear."

"Uh-huh." I turned all the way around in my seat to watch the SUV.

"What is it?" Chaz asked.

"Nothing," I lied. "Just trying to see who's in that thing."

"Is that tint street legal?" Burch asked.

Earp chuckled. "Who's going to pull them over? The Iraqi Highway Patrol?"

"Shut up, Earp," Burch said.

"It looks like Mongoose is about to pull that Claymore guy through the window of the driver's door!" Tabor called down from the turret.

Burch leaned out his window to see.

I pulled him back inside. "Eyes ahead. We've still got a job to do, and it's none of our business." But I smiled because we could hear the captain yelling.

"He's wasting his time. Claymore doesn't have to do anything he says," Earp said.

"And we need them," I added. "They've been where we're going and have a shared interest. Not to mention, we don't have enough bodies for a rescue mission."

A couple of minutes passed before my radio beeped again. "Punisher One, this is Mongoose. We're oscar mike. For any other vehicles we may encounter, Hammerhead says we are to stop and fire warning shots. Over."

"Roger that. Over." I looked at Burch. "Let's go."

SEVEN

We encountered only two more vehicles between Baheth and An Zahab. Thankfully, they both turned around and headed back to the city when we fired warning shots into the air. Their presence, racing away in the direction we were headed, was more confirmation that we were hopefully in the clear. Still, we kept our eyes open and our senses on high alert because nothing in war was ever guaranteed.

The city of An Zahab was more crowded than any of us would have liked with pedestrians, cars, and even livestock. A young man led a donkey and a goat down the side of the street.

I watched him wave at us through my scope.

Our convoy was rolling through the town at a snail's pace, but the locals moved out of our way without being asked. I scanned the danger areas, the rooftops and the windows that looked down on our path.

Black smoke was billowing into the sky from the road up ahead. I looked through the scope and saw a car burning in the distance. "Bet whatever blew that thing up was meant for us," I said to no one in particular.

As we passed the burning car, the heat radiating off it stung my face. People were yelling. There was a badly burned man lying in the ditch. We didn't stop.

We were all silent for a while, carefully combing our surroundings and the onlookers who flanked us. "Warren, my two o'clock. I don't like the looks of those hajjis over there watching us," Earp said from the back seat.

I panned across the vehicle to my left. "Slow down, Brayden."

Burch let off the gas.

Earp's suspicion was valid. Two men, one young and one old and both dressed in Western-style attire, watched us from beneath the overhang of a dilapidated building. The older of the two immediately caught my attention. He had short gray hair, was slightly overweight, and wore thick dark-rim glasses.

His soul was black as night. The kind of evil that had to be segregated in the toughest of prisons. Even from our distance, his wickedness made me shudder.

"Stop the car."

"Sir?" Burch asked.

"Stop the car!" I shouted.

The man locked eyes with me and stared. My hand went for the door handle, but I stopped, my better judgment kicking in. I clicked on my radio. "Mongoose, this is Punisher One. We've got two suspicious foot mobiles watching us from my two o'clock.

Requesting permission to question them. Over."

"Punisher One, this is Mongoose. Permission is denied. Your orders are to not stop on this highway. Over."

There was a reason that man was watching us the way he was. I turned my sights forward again and searched the area.

Burch leaned toward me. "Sir?"

"Don't move this vehicle."

"Sergeant Parish, we're under orders to move quickly through this city without stopping," Chaz said.

I ignored him. "Tabor, you see anything out of place up there?" I called toward the turret.

"No, sir, Sergeant. Just a bunch of Iraqis who are really grateful for their freedom."

Chaz grabbed my shoulder. "Sergeant Parish, I'm going to have to—"

My hand flew back in his face to silence him.

"Warren, man, you're making me nervous. What is it?" Earp asked, looking over my shoulder.

Just then, a black SUV pulled past us on the left. It was the new Claymore vehicle, the one that stirred all my senses.

"What the hell?" Chaz said.

The vehicle cut to the left, and the two men took off running. Every muscle in me twisted. I wanted to follow. I slammed my fist against the door.

"Parish, what do I do? Move out?" Burch asked.

Before I could answer, a motorbike sped by us on my right side. All our heads whipped in its direction.

Boom!

A wave of earth and pavement rose up three times the height of our Humvee, sending parts of the motorbike and its rider in every direction.

Burch threw his arm across my chest. "Whoa!"

"Holy shit!"

Our Humvee rocked to the side and came back down with a heavy thud. The windshield splintered. Rocks and dirt sprayed our roof. *Clink! Clink! Clink!* Smoke and dust rolled around us.

"IED! IED!" I yelled into my radio, like they couldn't have seen it themselves.

"Get the hell out of there!" someone yelled back.

I grabbed Burch's shoulder and shoved him forward. "Gas! Go! Go! Go!"

Brayden threw the transmission in gear and the vehicle lurched forward. I gripped the door, silently praying that we weren't about to race through a minefield. Gunfire rattled through the air. It was an ambush.

Tabor, in the turret, fired back.

Bullets ripped through the metal around us.

"Go! Go!"

We hit a pothole that threw us all into the ceiling of the Humvee. My helmet clanged against it making lights dance in the corners of my eyes. The gunfire waned as we raced through the city.

I was finally able to turn and look at my guys. "Everyone OK? Anybody hit?"

"All good, Sergeant," Tabor called down, giving us a thumbs-up.

"Good," Burch panted, his eyes wide.

Earp let out a loud *"Yeehaw!"*

My head was spinning, and there was a loud ringing in my right ear. I looked around for the new Claymore SUV and didn't see it anywhere.

Earp smacked the back of my helmet. "How the hell did you know what was up?"

"Me? It was you. You called it back there."

"Yeah, but you've got like some voodoo sixth sense, Sergeant." Earp shook his head and laughed. "Holy fuck that was crazy."

"Punisher One, everybody whole up there?" Headley asked over my radio.

"All good here. Our vehicle took quite a bit of fire. We'll need to check it out once we get somewhere safe. Over."

"Punisher Two sustained fire as well. No injuries. Over," Pearson said.

"Chuckwagon is all clear."

"We're all clear too if anyone cares," Huffman responded from the other Claymore car.

I laughed, adrenaline pumping through

my veins and lighting every nerve ending inside me on fire. Nothing like a close brush with death to make you feel alive.

Earp howled out the window again.

We made it to the other side of An Zahab without further incident and stopped outside the city to inventory the damage. Our vehicle had taken the most gunfire, and it had shredded our right front tire. I stood back and watched as Earp and Burch argued about how best to change it.

"You saved our asses out there today," Chaz said, walking up beside me with his rifle resting across his chest. "I'm sorry about my mistake with Chavez."

I nodded.

"And I shouldn't have questioned you in front of your men. I apologize for that too."

"Still, you were right. I'm not supposed to question orders."

"Warren, if you hadn't questioned our orders, every man in our vehicle would be dead. You know it."

I put my hand on his shoulder and squeezed. "But we're not."

"Thanks to you."

"Thanks to Earp. He saw them first."

Chaz was staring at me. Then he took a step forward and lowered his voice. "How did you know?"

I sighed. "A wicked sixth sense, I guess."

That was about the closest I'd ever come to telling a brother the truth.

"Warren, a word?" Headley called behind us.

I swore under my breath.

"Good luck," Chaz mumbled.

I followed the captain back to his vehicle, where he stopped and turned to face me. He was quiet for a second, choosing his words carefully—a rare ability in our profession. He crossed his hulking arms over his chest. "How did you know?"

Popular question.

I tapped my fingers on my rifle. "Earp saw the men. They looked suspicious. When we slowed, the way the guy was looking at me...it was pretty obvious something was off."

He cut his eyes at me.

I shifted awkwardly on my feet. "Sir, I was simply following procedure. The men looked suspicious, like they were waiting to pull a trigger or watch a bomb go off. Any of us could have seen it."

He looked around to make sure we were out of earshot of anyone else. "But you're always the guy to know. Why is that, Parish?"

I chuckled. "I'd like to know that myself, Captain."

And that was the honest-to-god truth. No one wanted to know why I was the way I was more than me.

It was clear Headley wanted to ask more personal questions, but he didn't. I relaxed a little. "You still think we should bypass the south entrance, circle around and go in from the north?"

"Or the east. Pearson was right. We could take that side street in on the east."

"I wonder what kind of defense they have on the roads," he said.

"Claymore mentioned a chain-link fence on the south. It could form a perimeter."

He glanced over my shoulder toward the Claymore SUV. "Think you could find out if they know anything else?"

I nodded. "Are you going to call it in to Hammerhead?"

"I'd better. Our luck, we wouldn't, and someone would order an air strike."

I chuckled. "I've thought the same thing myself."

"Find out what you can. Then let me know. I'm going to find a way off this highway, and call it in to command. I'll call a team meeting when I know more."

"Roger that, Captain."

I turned and walked back to Claymore's SUV. Fury was in the passenger seat, her hair blowing backward on the breeze from the car's vents. I knocked on the glass. She rolled down the window and the foreign chill of air conditioning rattled my wits.

I shook my head to clear it. "Excuse me, ma'am. Can I—"

"You can shut the hell up with that *ma'am* shit is what you can do."

I couldn't suppress a smile. "My apologies. Can I ask you a question?"

"You just did, Sergeant."

"How much of that compound did you see yesterday?" I asked, ignoring her snark.

She crossed her arms. "Is this the Marine Corps asking for the help of a lowly contractor?"

"This is *me* asking."

She studied my face for a moment. "In that case…" She turned and reached behind the empty driver's seat into the seat-back pocket. Then she handed me a small stack of surveillance photos. "Would these help?"

"Holy shit. Yeah, these will help." There were a handful of pictures of the compound where the weapons were being stored. I'd only seen aerials of them before, but these showed gates, doors, windows, and guards.

She tapped the top photo of the gray warehouse's exterior. "Isn't this what Recon is supposed to do?"

"Yeah. Unfortunately, this isn't the average Recon mission."

She looked behind me. "I can tell. You guys look like a bunch of grunts."

"Don't get me started." The third photo in the stack showed one long side of the metal fence. "What's the length of this fence? Does it go all the way around?"

"Pretty sure. Well, it used to. We drove through the front side of it."

"Know anything about a road on the

east side?"

She nodded. "There's a paved road, but it runs through a pretty populated area. You'll have to get through their quickly, or you'll run the risk of locals calling in your approach to people inside the compound."

"We still need to do this after dark."

"Bet your ass you do. Was there a question?"

I just lifted an eyebrow.

She laughed and shook her head. "Who the hell is running this mission?"

"A major hoping to make major general before the next budget term."

"Explains a lot."

I stuck out my hand toward her. "Hey, thanks a lot for the intel."

She put her hand in mine. It was surprisingly soft given her rock-hard exterior —and personality. "Anytime, Warren."

God, I loved the sound of my name in her mouth. Liked it too much. I held onto her for a second longer than I should have, staring at her lips like some kind of douche.

I was saved by the familiar grinding of tires on desert turf. I blinked and released her. She pushed her door open and got out. "That would be us."

I shielded my eyes against the sun fading over the horizon and saw the sleek black unmarked SUV. "Sure as shit isn't property of the US government. Not enough rattling and peeling paint."

"Maybe you should join us on the dark side." She slammed her door, then adjusted the assault rifle resting between her breasts. "See you later, Sergeant."

I caught her arm and nodded toward the vehicle. "Who's in that?"

Her jaw tightened just enough for me to notice. "Part of our other team that was collecting intel in An Zahab."

She was lying.

"You already had your guy, at least up

until we helped you lose him. Why would you need more intel in the city?"

"That's classified."

"Sure it is."

She looked down at where my hand was holding her arm. I released it, then stood there and shamefully watched her walk away. She probably knew I was looking, given the exaggerated sweep of her ass from side to side.

"They don't make 'em like that where I come from," Burch said quietly. I hadn't even realized he'd walked up beside me.

I kept my thoughts to myself.

She walked to the back door behind the driver, and whoever was inside rolled down the window. I caught a flash of a person on the other side of the glass before Fury stepped in to block my discerning view. I pinched the corners of my tired eyes and looked again.

Whoever she was talking to was

completely out of my view, but not off my radar. I could feel their presence, even from fifty yards away.

No one exited the vehicle. I wondered if they'd caught the men we'd seen in the city, and if they had, what had become of them. Had it been me, I wouldn't have brought the older one back alive.

"What have you got there?" Burch asked, leaning close to me.

I handed him the photos Fury had given me. "Our target. Compliments of our unlikely comrades."

"You got these from Claymore?"

I nodded.

He slowly shook his head as he flipped through them. "Sometimes I wonder what we're doing out here at all."

I grinned over at him. "Cheap labor, my friend."

"Isn't that the truth? I bet one of Claymore's guys is worth about five of us."

"More like ten." I'd done the math. I knew.

Fury glanced back over her shoulder and looked at me. I still couldn't see past her, but I knew I was now the subject of her conversation. Then the window rolled up, all the way up, before she turned and walked toward her own car.

Burch handed me back the photos. "You're going to make Hammerhead's day with these."

"Hey, is there anything weird to you about that car?" I asked, already knowing his answer before he gave it.

His head fell to the side. "No. It looks like what POTUS rides in."

"I don't think that's the president." But I certainly didn't know who it was. I nudged his arm and turned around to head back to our convoy. "Come on. I need to talk to the captain."

Headley was stepping out of his Humvee

when we approached. I held up the photos. "I come bearing gifts."

Burch elbowed my arm. "I'm going to go check on that tire."

I nodded.

The captain took the photos from me. "What's this?"

"Pictures that *we* should have taken."

He flipped through them. "No shit."

"No shit." I pointed to the side of one of the pictures. "Here's our entrance, but Claymore said—"

"You mean *Fury* said." The corner of his mouth tipped up in a knowing grin.

"Yes. *Fury* said the side road is through a populated area. We need to slip in there after dark so there's less chance of the locals giving the bad guys a heads-up. What's the word from Hammerhead?"

"We're clear to go around and get off the main highway."

"That's good."

"It's a miracle, you mean."

I chuckled. "Yeah."

He jerked his chin toward the Claymore vehicles. "Do you know if they caught those guys they went after?"

I really wished I did. "I don't, but I haven't seen anyone come or go from that SUV. Think we could search it?" Had I been a superstitious guy, I would've crossed my fingers behind my back, hoping Headley would say yes.

He didn't. "As much as I hate to admit it, I think we're going to need them on our side when this goes down. Better not do anything to piss them off." He swirled a finger around in the air. "Help me get everyone gathered around. Team meeting time."

"Yes, sir."

"Huddle up!" I shouted.

Everyone on our mission gathered around us by the command vehicle. Five of the contractors from Claymore, including

Fury, stood close enough to hear. Both of their SUVs had rolled closer to our convoy.

War was near. My heart rate had picked up, and the hair was standing on the back of my neck. I tightened my grip on my rifle.

Headley turned to face us all. "Shit just got real, gentleman." He cast a stern look over our group. "But now it's time to show this enemy why the US government sent us in to deal with them. We are the reckoning that awaits. We are the axe delivered to cut the head off this snake."

A few "Oorah"s floated around the team.

"In the past forty-eight hours, the IJS opened fire on our convoy, attacked us in our sleep, attempted to blow us all to kingdom come with an IED, and abducted one of our men. Now it's our time to show them how royally they fucked up by failing in their attempts to take us out when they had the chance.

"Our top priority tonight is to rescue Lance Corporal Nick Chavez. But in addition to that, we're also about to execute a raid on the last standing hub of insurgent activity here in northern Iraq. Destroying this establishment will cripple the entire IJS operation."

My head was humming with excitement.

"Our plans of attack have changed. We're going to head east off this highway and avoid any further surprises the IJS may have planned for us. Our intelligence shows a dirt road that leads into the southeastern portion of the city. It will be past sundown by the time we arrive, and once we're there, we'll haul ass through a highly residential area to hit the compound from the east side."

I realized Headley seemed to be speaking over our heads. His plan-of-attack speech was for Claymore's benefit even more than ours.

"A chain-link fence forms a perimeter around the complex. When we get there, we'll fan out and lay down fire from the .50 Cals while we plow through that fence. This is a full-frontal assault. All enemy targets are declared hostile, but one of our guys is in there, so you'd better know who you're shooting at."

"Captain!" someone called out behind us. Everyone turned to look. It was Enzo. "They have quite the firepower on the first floor of that building. I don't recommend going in throwing grenades, or you might set off a daisy chain by accident."

Headley's expression was pinched, but he nodded. After all, he wasn't stupid. "Thank you. Did you guys hear that? Their stash is on the ground level, and we already know they're making bombs."

He pointed at me. "Punisher One will be on point." After a thoughtful second, he looked over our heads again. "And

Claymore will bring up the rear."

Whispers fluttered through our group. An alliance of this sort was unprecedented to say the least. I looked back to see Enzo nodding. Headley was smiling. And Fury was looking at me.

"This raid-and-rescue operation is going to be textbook in its execution, meaning this will be a swift takedown of the installation with complete destruction of the enemy asset. The mission will end with a successful withdrawal and return back to base. We *will* go home with *every* single person we came here with, and by this time tomorrow, we'll all have hot showers and a good night's sleep in a real bed."

That elicited a lot of applause.

"I want to thank you all for being patriots. For being Marines. And for being the swift, silent, deadly dogs of this war."

"Oorah!" a few Marines said together.

Headley smiled. "Now, who's ready to go

blow some shit up?"

EIGHT

Every nerve ending inside me was humming as we rolled into the city at a quarter past dark. Adrenaline was a drug, one we'd all been hopped up on since well before we landed in the country. It had never been so strong for me as it was this night, except for maybe the time in Afghanistan two years before.

In stark contrast to An Zahab, the outskirts of Tuz Sehir were quiet. Large concrete walls separated the houses from the streets. Most were splashed with Arabic graffiti, seemingly marked as if someone was claiming ownership of them. I recognized the sign for the IJS on some. The farther we got into the city, the more buildings were burned or reduced to rubble.

We were certainly in the right place.

A few pedestrians gave us sideways glances as we tore through the streets, but we didn't slow in case any of them planned to alert the terrorists inside the compound.

After a couple of turns, a large light-colored structure came into view about six hundred meters ahead. "Is that it?" Burch asked.

I strained through my NVGs, the green glow distorting the terrain. Its silhouette looked the same as the building in the photos. But I didn't see a fence; there looked to be a concrete wall instead.

I clicked on my radio. "Mongoose, this is Punisher One. We've got the building in sight, but I think it's surrounded by a concrete wall instead of a fence."

Burch slammed his fist against the steering wheel. "This is why you don't rely on goddamn contractors for intel! We should have done that shit ourselves!"

"Is there a gate?" Headley replied quickly.

We were getting closer. "Negative, sir. Not from what I can see."

My radio beeped again almost immediately. "Mongoose, Punisher, whoever the hell is listening up there, move to the right shoulder and Claymore will take the lead. Over." It was a deep voice that sounded oddly familiar.

Well, shit.

I waited, and Burch slowed the Humvee.

My radio beeped after what felt like an eternity. "Punisher One, this is Mongoose Actual. Move to the right shoulder."

"Burch, pull to the right. Claymore's

taking the lead," I said.

"Damn!" Earp shouted in the back seat.

"I'll bet that shit won't be called up to command," Burch said as he pulled to the right side of the road and almost came to a complete stop.

The two Claymore SUVs sped past us on the left. Burch quickly punched the gas to keep up with them, but before our tire tread could even successfully grab the pavement, a loud blast made Burch swerve.

I clapped my hands over my ears and looked for an IED explosion. There was no fireball or flash, but there was what looked to be a shockwave bowling forward toward the building and…

BOOM!

The wall's explosion was so fierce that our Humvee lurched like we'd hit an invisible speed bump. I grabbed the dashboard to keep from slamming my head against it. Earp wasn't so lucky. He face-planted into the back of Burch's seat, then screamed out in pain and cursed.

Our Humvee was pelted with rocks and dirt.

"Tabor, you OK?" I shouted up toward the turret.

"Yeah, what the fuck was that?" he yelled back.

I had no idea.

My radio went off. "Was that an RPG?" someone asked, as breathless as we all were.

"That was Claymore, I think. But I have no idea what the hell they did," I answered.

"Claymore?" Mongoose asked over the radio.

"That was a little magic, boys." It was Fury speaking. "Follow us."

Up ahead, Claymore's taillights were still moving through the cloud of smoke. We followed them.

Pop! Pop! Pop!

Gunfire rattled through the air, lighting

the night sky with bright green flashes. Tabor fired back as we plowed through what was left of the concrete wall. Burch followed the taillights in front of us to the right through some kind of courtyard.

It wasn't until the Claymore SUV spun toward the building, prompting us to do the same, that I realized only Fury's car was in front of us. The mysterious Claymore SUV that had been in front of her, had gone left when we entered to bookend our Humvees in a straight line.

Four fresh dead bodies were already laying in front of us.

Gunfire exploded from all of our turrets at the shooters on the roof and in the second-story windows. The rest of us got out behind our doors and fired at the shooters on the ground.

When it was clear enough, I shouted back to Earp. "Earp, cover us!"

"Roger that, Sergeant!"

And just like that, Jessica Rabbit popped into my head. *Fucking Earp.*

I motioned to Burch. "Let's go!"

All but a handful of us teamed up and pushed toward the building. Earp stayed back with Tabor. Enzo, Huffman, and Fury stacked up with me, Burch, and Chaz. Fury went in on point. I was right behind her, *nut to butt*, as we say in the military.

The door appeared to have been forced open earlier, probably by Claymore. Someone had done a half-assed job of securing it with a metal latch and a padlock.

Huffman stepped forward with a twelve-gauge shotgun and blew off the door latch. Then he stepped to the back of our line.

I moved to the right, and Fury pushed the door in, opening the fatal funnel of the doorway. A man was aiming a handgun at us. She took him down with a round of quick bursts from her 5.56.

My eyes scanned the floor for tripwires

or other booby traps as we moved inside. Another man ran into the room with an AK-47, and I dropped him just as he pulled the trigger. Bullets from his gun peppered the ceiling.

I panned the room with my rifle. Mortar shells used for making IEDs, hundreds of them, were stacked along the side of the room beside a staircase.

Headley and his team passed by us. He patted my shoulder. "Clear upstairs!" he shouted over the gunfire outside.

I nodded, and started in that direction. The rest of my team followed. Fury went up the stairs first. A man peeked around the corner at the top. She fired, and he ducked back out of view.

The narrow stairs landed on the second floor in a large room with four open doors leading off it. Fury and I ascended into it almost back to back. There were targets in all the rooms. She fired left and I fired right as we hurried to get out of the way for more help to join us.

Then two men ran through two different doors on my side of the room. As I shot the guy on my left, the other guy fired at me before Burch took him down.

The bullet slammed into my right side, doubling me over and knocking the air from my lungs. I felt my ribs crack under the impact. Burch came over top of me and fired into the room, dropping a third Iraqi to the floor.

Someone grabbed the back of my shirt, pulled me upright, and pushed me forward. Chaz.

Heaving and barely able to see because of the tears in my eyes, I forced myself back in line in front of him. I quickly slid my fingers along my armored side to check for blood. There wasn't any. I straightened as much as possible and focused on what was around the next corner.

In a room full of assault rifles, some Russian-made and some American, Chaz and I returned fire on two men shooting from behind a table.

Fury and Enzo were firing through an open door into the next room. We all followed her. Except for the lifeless bodies on the floor and more ammo than I'd ever seen in one place that size, the room was empty. On the other side of it was a closed door. We carefully made our way across, with Chaz and Huffman watching our back at the door we'd come in.

Downstairs and outside, the gunshots were slowing.

We pushed through toward the back door, stepping over bodies and RPGs. Fury tried the door handle and shook her head. She stepped back, and I sprayed the handle with bullets, carefully aimed toward the wall since we didn't know who was on the other side.

She pushed it open, and I shot a man who was charging toward us. The room was a dead end. Only two other people were inside. Chavez, who was very much alive, and Claymore's lost captive. He was still wearing a polo shirt. It was now covered in blood.

All guns were aimed at where he was slumped against the wall on the floor. An AK was laying just out of his reach and blood bubbled out of his mouth.

I quickly stepped toward him, screaming for him to show me his hands in the little bit of broken Arabic that I knew.

He didn't move, but his eyes locked with mine. One of his was black; the other was deep blue.

He gasped, nearly choking on the blood, but almost looked...relieved? Excited? Then he began sputtering words, most of which I couldn't understand. Then he said *mukhbir* several times. That one I knew. It meant "informant."

He suddenly reached toward me. "Azr ___"

And Enzo fired twice, putting two bullets into his skull.

There was silence all around us. No more gunfire. No more screaming. Chavez was shaking on the floor, beaten and gagged, but otherwise, seemingly, OK.

Neither the Marines nor Claymore suffered any fatalities, even though several of us had been shot. A bullet tore clean through Fradera's right bicep. A Claymore operator was grazed across the thigh. And I had taken a round—thankfully from a handgun—to the chest. It broke my ribs, but it didn't penetrate my body armor. I would certainly live.

I couldn't say as much for the IJS.

Every IJS member in the compound was dead, including Claymore's target, Yazen al-

Zawbai. He had been shot through the window as he fired on our men outside, then finished off by Enzo when we reached him upstairs.

Too bad I couldn't have asked him some questions.

Crippled by the pain burning through my side, I limped out of the building, determined to get some answers out of the second Claymore vehicle. But when I walked out, it was gone.

"Warren, are you hit?" Doc called out as he bandaged Fradera's upper arm.

"Yeah, but not through the skin." When I reached him, I finally stripped off my gear and body armor. The adrenaline was leaving my bloodstream, intensifying the pain with each second. I unbuttoned my blouse and eased my arms out of it. By the time I pulled up my undershirt, a crowd had gathered.

"Oh!"

"Fuck, man!"

"Whoa!"

"Ouch!"

Burch grabbed my shoulder. "Damn, man."

A goose egg had ballooned up over my blackened ribcage on my right side. I swore a few times and bit down on my knuckles as the shock of it settled in.

Doc leaned down for a closer look. "You've got some broken ribs."

I was still wincing. "No shit."

"Where were you when this happened?" he asked.

"Second floor, top of the stairs. The guy was maybe twenty feet away," I said.

"Weren't you outside when Headley moved in?"

"Nope."

"I swear I thought you were over by command's vehicle."

Burch chuckled and nudged my arm. "That's why we started calling him Shadow in Afghanistan. It's like there's always two of him."

"You know I hate that name," I said through a groan.

"Come here," Doc said to me as he put on his stethoscope. I stepped over beside him, and he put the cool round chest piece on the front of my good lung first. "Take a deep breath."

"No," I said with a pained grin.

"Quit being a pussy, Sergeant. Deep breath. Come on."

I breathed in, my eyes watering some more. "God, that hurts."

"We're going to have to do it again. I couldn't hear shit."

I rolled my eyes.

"Everybody, shut the hell up!" Doc shouted to the guys standing around us.

"Better yet"—Headley pushed his way through the onlookers around me—"if you're not on watch or waiting to see Doc, get your asses back to the supply truck and start unloading our gear. We need to blow that building and get the hell out of this shithole."

"Aww," Burch whined. "We were taking bets to see if Parish would cry."

I reached out to punch him in the shoulder and immediately regretted it.

Laughing as I winced, he backed away. "Make sure it's *deep*, princess," he taunted.

I shot him the bird.

"Breathe again," Doc said when they were gone.

I obeyed, and he listened to the front and back of my good lung first. He moved the stethoscope down below the injury. "Again." I breathed, and then he moved the stethoscope to my back. "One more time."

I took another breath as deep as I could manage.

"I don't hear any holes, which is good. You need an X-ray though." He looked up at Headley. "He probably needs to head back on the helo with Fradera and Chavez."

I lowered my shirt. "That's really not necessary. We'll finish up here, and I'll ride back with my guys."

Doc shook his head. "I really don't recommend it. You know those big bumps we took here? Depending on how many of these bad boys are busted"—he nodded to my chest—"one of them could pop out and puncture your lung or your aorta."

Headley put his hand on my shoulder. "You're going with the others. No sense in taking the chance."

I opened my mouth to argue, but Headley gave me a look that dared me to speak. I sighed, and it hurt. "Roger that, sir."

"We'll see you back at camp. Get some rest. You've earned it." He extended his hand to shake mine. "Good work today."

"Thank you, sir."

He turned and walked back to the

supply truck.

"Warren," Fury said behind me.

I slowly turned. She was walking over from her SUV. "Nice work in there tonight. I'll admit I was skeptical, but I'd fight alongside you any day," I said.

"Skeptical because I'm a woman?"

I smiled. "Because you're a civilian."

She laughed. "Fair enough. How's the side?"

"I imagine this is what being run over by a tank might feel like." I pulled my shirt up. The purplish black over my ribs had deepened even more.

She sucked in a sharp breath through her teeth. "Geez."

"Yeah." I put my shirt down. "I'm about to get an airlift out of here though."

"Good."

"Your guy upstairs. Yazen whatever. His eyes"—I pointed to my own—"they were mismatched too."

She smiled. "Think it's a conspiracy?"

"He said he was an informant."

That gave her pause.

"Who was he an informant for? Us or _you_?"

"I don't know what you're talking about."

She was lying again.

"Who was in the other SUV?"

"You already asked me that."

"This time, I want you to tell me the truth."

The corner of her mouth tipped up in a half smile. "Maybe someday, but not tonight."

"You think I'll see you after this?"

She took a step toward me. "I know I will."

I swallowed. Hard.

And without another word, she turned and walked away.

When she was gone, I went back to

collect my gear I'd dropped on the ground. That was when I noticed Chavez sitting halfway in and halfway out of the back seat of Doc's Humvee. I walked over to him, still holding my side. "Nick?"

He didn't look at me. The whole left side of his face was swollen, and his left eyebrow was split open and crusted with blood. His lip was busted, and his nose was broken. He was cradling his arm across his chest and staring out the window.

"Nick, you all right?" I asked again.

One rogue tear streaked through the dirt on his puffy cheek.

Doc stepped over beside me and turned so that his back was to Chavez. He lowered his voice. "He can't answer you very easily. Pretty sure his jaw is broken. His shoulder was dislocated too, but I reset it, and all the bones in his right hand were crushed."

I hadn't even noticed how mangled his fingers were. "Anything life threatening?" I asked, wondering how my presence might affect him.

"Not that I can tell, but he's not communicating much with me either. It's like he's catatonic."

"Did you give him drugs?"

"Morphine, just a few minutes ago, but he was like this from the moment he came out. The IJS worked him over pretty hard."

"I'm glad they're dead."

"Me too, man. You good?"

"Yeah. Thanks. I'm going to get my shit, and I'll be right back."

I gathered my stuff and carried the load back to where Chavez was still staring off in the same direction as when I left him. Dropping my gear on the ground, I sat down in the dirt beside Chavez's leg. He might not talk to me, but he needed to know I was there and not going to leave him.

That was when I realized his right boot on the ground was poised, ready to run. I sat close enough that my shoulder barely touched his shaking calf. After a second, I felt it relax, even if only slightly.

I leaned my head back against the vehicle. Closed my eyes on the stars above and whispered into the night, "We're going home."

NINE

Back on base there were only four things in the world I wanted: heavy drugs, a hot shower, clean underwear, and sleep. In that order. I almost scored them perfectly too, except when I was finally released from the hospital and made it to the bath house, my eyes closed for a second in the shower.

You've never known exhaustion until you've dozed off standing up, with your forehead leaned against a grimy shower wall covered with the body sludge of a thousand sweaty men.

My knees buckled, jolting me awake before I fell to the floor.

When I finally hit my sheets, I was sucked under the weight of unconsciousness like a swimmer lost to a tsunami. Despite the broken ribs, I didn't dream. I didn't move. I never even bothered with a blanket.

Thank God for narcotics.

Had it not been for a loud knock at my door sometime later, I might never have woken up. When I did, I wished I hadn't. My chest felt like someone had dropped a guillotine on it in my sleep.

Before moving, I reached to the nightstand for my bottle of painkillers and my watch. It was just after 1700 hours, well past time for my next round of meds. I stuck one in my mouth, swallowing it dry.

Whoever was at my door knocked again.

The towel I'd tacked up over the window had partially fallen, so the Iraqi sun blinded me when I forced myself up to sitting. I took a few swigs from my water bottle and braced myself for the agony of standing.

"Holy shit," I said with a groan.

As if a gunshot wound wasn't enough, pain melted down my spine and pooled throughout my hips as I straightened. Part of the consequences of shitty Humvee road trips and lugging around a hundred pounds worth of gear.

I swore as I walked barefoot across the room in my black boxer briefs, then pulled the door open just enough to peek outside.

Fury.

She had showered and changed into a fresh pair of desert-cam cargo pants and an olive-drab tank top. Her long black hair was braided over one shoulder, and she wore dark sunglasses. She lowered them to look at me. "Morning, sunshine."

My eyes scanned the grounds behind her. Thankfully, my trailer faced the back of another one, and no one seemed to be around. "What are you doing here?"

"It's a thousand degrees in this sun, Warren. Can I come in?"

Panic constricted my heart. "Not allowed."

Her head tilted. "Seriously?"

Shit. "Give me a sec."

I slammed the door and flipped on the light. Moving carefully, I grabbed a pair of PT shorts off the shelf at the foot of my bed. When I bent to put them on, I thought I might die—or at least pass out. Had it been *anyone* else in all of Iraq, I wouldn't have bothered. As it was, there was no way in hell I was letting that woman anywhere near me while I was wearing nothing but a pair of fitted black boxer briefs. That is…not unless she was prepared to do something about it, of course.

Next, I reached for the bottle of mouthwash in my shower bag that I'd thankfully left on top of my mini fridge. I took a long swig and swished it around while I looked for a place to spit it out. My tiny trailer didn't have a sink or its own bathroom, so I spit it right back into the bottle, then tossed the whole thing in the trash.

The room smelled like six days of ball sweat and dirt from my pile of rancid clothes heaped in the corner. I kicked them under my bed, then reached for the can of air freshener on my narrow bookshelf.

Fury walked in as I was hosing down the room with a thick layer of citrus breeze.

She coughed and covered her mouth as she closed the door behind her. "Knock it off. You're making that shit infinitely worse."

"I guarantee you, I'm not." I put the can back down and turned toward her as she removed her sunglasses. She hooked them on the front of her tank top—right into the center valley that I found so terribly distracting. "You're not supposed to be in here."

"I know."

Her eyes fell to my chest, and she took a step toward me. "Holy hell, Warren. That's awful."

I looked down. From just below my right peck, down to almost level with my belly button, the area was solid blackish purple.

"Trust me, it feels even worse than it looks."

"I don't doubt it."

She looked above the bruising to the tattoo across my chest, then reached up and traced her finger along its edge. "This is impressive."

A lump rose in my throat as chill bumps rippled my skin under her touch. "Thank you."

Her finger followed the thick black lines over my shoulder, and she stepped beside me for a better look at the rest of the tattoo that stretched across my back. Her eyes narrowed. "Is that…?"

"Dragon claws."

She relaxed and laughed.

"Why? What did you think it was?" I asked.

She smiled. "Demon claws."

I stepped away from her and plucked a white T-shirt from the shelf. "What are you doing here, Fury?"

"Am I making you uncomfortable?"

"No." *Yes.* I pulled the shirt over my head and winced as I stuck my good arm through it. When I tried my arm on my bad side, I couldn't raise it higher than my shoulder.

"Just stop," she said.

I froze, halfway in and out of my shirt.

She walked toward me again and carefully pulled the T-shirt back off, letting her hands slide across the back of my neck and all the way down my good arm. She tossed the shirt onto my bed. "Do you have anything with buttons?"

I raked my hand through my short hair and walked to the particle-board box that served as a closet. Inside was the gray shirt I'd worn the night we flew out.

She reached for it. "Let me help?"

I handed it to her and she slipped the sleeve over my bad arm first. "Have you ever been shot before?"

"No," I said as she stepped dangerously close to pull the shirt around my back. "Have you?"

"A year and a half ago in Kosovo. A five-five-six hit my plates in the back." She helped me put my good arm into the other sleeve. "Thankfully, it didn't do any permanent damage to my spine, but it did break a few ribs, so I know how you feel."

I wasn't so sure that was true. I'd never been so turned on and in so much pain in my life. Thank God I'd put on shorts.

"How did you get here so fast?" I asked,

desperately needing to think about something else.

She buttoned the third button down on my shirt. "Claymore sent in a replacement team to drive back. They flew my team out just after you left."

My brow lifted as her hands moved down. "You had a shift change...in the field?"

"Yes. Jealous?"

"A little bit," I said with a chuckle, followed by a wince.

"I don't recommend laughing for a few weeks."

I smiled, watching her hands work the button over my stomach. "It doesn't happen often."

She gripped the front of my shirt. "All done. Wasn't that easier?"

"Much. Thank you."

When she didn't immediately move away, my hands twitched at my sides. It was all I could do to not grab her and pull her against me, broken ribs or not.

Then she stepped back and sat down on my bed. *Gulp.* She patted the seat beside her. I shook my head and didn't budge, partly because the transitions between standing and sitting were agonizing. And partly because I didn't trust either of us.

"I want to offer you a job," she said, crossing her legs.

"I have a job."

"What if we could pull some strings to get you out?"

Was this chick serious? "No offense, but who do you think you are? Lady Liberty? I work for the US Marine Corps, not exactly the sort of career you can hand in a two weeks' notice for."

"We've done it before. We could do it again." She cocked an eyebrow. "Would you be interested?"

Would I be interested in the time off?

The paycheck? And the air transport to fly me out of hostile territory at the end of my work day? Hell yeah.

But I shook my head. "I'm not going to leave my guys."

"That's respectable. And stupid."

"Call it what you want. But that's my decision."

She stared at me for a second. "You wanna know who was in the other SUV last night?"

I shifted on my feet. "Yes, but it's not going to change my mind."

"It was Damon Claymore."

I blinked. "*The* Damon Claymore? As in Claymore Worldwide? Owner of the largest private army in the world?"

She nodded.

Nobody I knew had ever seen the elusive CEO. Heard about him, sure. He was an absolute legend as one of the most decorated soldiers in the Gulf War. But had anyone actually seen him? I'd heard rumors that even photos of him didn't exist. Damon Claymore was a ghost.

"How'd he take down that wall? There was no flash from an explosive or anything."

She smiled. "Oh, honey, we have access to weapons the US government can't even dream of."

"And he was really there?"

She nodded. "That's right. My command showed up in the field last night to help us. And he's still in the area. How's the authority situation around here?"

Calvin hadn't crossed my mind much less my path since I arrived back on base. Not even at the hospital. Not even for Chavez, someone taken prisoner and almost killed under his watch.

I pressed my eyes closed to reset my thoughts. My responsibility wasn't to Calvin. It was to my men.

Fury continued. "That kind of

leadership, plus a six-figure paycheck. What's the problem here, Warren?"

"I made a commitment. And I'm going to honor it."

With a sigh, she bowed her head slightly. "I can respect that." She stood again. "Maybe after your contract is up."

I nodded. "Maybe."

"You're done in two years?"

"Almost."

She twisted a button on the front of my shirt again and cut her eyes at me. "That's a long time." Her voice was now soft…Her eyes too.

Maybe the painkillers were starting to make me feel lightheaded.

Then she touched her lips to mine, and I was sure I had to be high on something. I flinched away. Then my gaze fell to her mouth as she trapped the side of her lower lip between her teeth.

"Fuck it," I said, stepping into her before

my better judgment could talk me out of it. I grabbed her waist and pulled her hips against mine, bending until tears sprang to my eyes and my mouth crashed down on hers.

Everything in me twisted in agony.

And in pleasure.

I slid my arm around her back to pull her up and tighter against me. And when I did, a rib shifted enough to make me cry out in pain.

She put her hands on both sides of my face and cringed along with me. "I'm sorry, Warren."

"No, I'm sorry," I said through a groan. "God, I don't think I've ever wanted anyone more than I want you right here, right now."

"I know the feeling." Smiling, she slid her hands down to mine, squeezed them, and let them go. "Get better, Sergeant. I expect you to be whole the next time we meet."

"I will be. And you'd better believe I'm picking up right where I'm leaving off."

She walked to the door, then smiled back over her shoulder. "Roger that, Sergeant."

And just like that, I would never think of Jessica Rabbit again.

THANK YOU FOR READING!

★ ★ ★ ★ ★

Please consider leaving a review on Amazon! Reviews help other readers discover new books.

Warren Parish is one of the leading men in the wildly popular series, The Soul Summoner.

THE SOUL SUMMONER SERIES

BRITCHES GET STITCHES

A Music City Rollers Novel

ONE

The whole house smelled like eggs.

Not the best way to start off girls' night. I threw open the sliding glass door letting the cold Nashville night air rush into the house. Sure, the gas heat was going right out into the neighborhood, but did I care? Nope. No longer my bill. No longer my problem. I pushed open a few windows too.

Heavy paws thudded down the hallway as the sliding wheels of the patio door announced canine freedom throughout the house. Bodhi bounded past me, water dripping from his golden snout. He'd probably been drinking from the half-bath toilet again, his preferred water bowl over the expensive filtered fountain I'd had installed in the laundry room.

As I drank the last drop of the 2013 Chateau St. Jean Cinq Cépages we'd been saving for a special occasion, I watched Bodhi romp unbridled through our backyard. Well, Clay's backyard. Err... Make that Clay and *Ginny's* backyard.

Dr. Virginia "Ginny" Allen, M.D.— or as my friends and I had taken to calling her, "Dr. Vagina"—was the cardiologist now, quite obviously, occupying my bed. Lab coats and mall-bought dresses hung in my closet, and a Ph.D*iva* mug sat by the coffeemaker.

Bitch. I hoped she *was* a diva.

In hindsight, I should've seen the affair coming. But to my embarrassment, I'd sexistly assumed "Dr. Allen" was a man for the first few months my husband rattled on about her:

"Grace, you would love Dr. Allen in the new TennStar office."

"Dr. Allen told me the funniest story about a patient today."

And, oh let's not forget: "Grace, you and Dr. Allen would really hit it off. You've got so much in common."

Yes. The same shitty taste in men, apparently.

I tried to drink from the glass again, but alas, still empty. I leaned on the doorway for support. Emotional and vertical.

Bodhi lifted his leg on the corner of Clay's toolshed. I appreciated the canine solidarity.

The backyard had always been my favorite part of the house. With the vintage lights strung between the ancient oak trees and the vine-draped pergola built by my father's own hands, it could have been a fairy's paradise. Ripped straight from the pages of *A Midsummer Night's Dream*.

Our first year in the house, Clay and I had spent the warm summer evenings snuggling on the wicker chaise lounge under the pergola. Me sprawled against his side, my head on his chest as he read to me.

The Martyr's Wife by C. E. Frost had been our favorite. That wine-soaked memory now so acute I could almost feel the warmth of his breath against my blonde hair as he'd read aloud. "*This moment in time is ours, completely ours. Even if for but a moment, I will hold you as though the light of the sun may not burn tomorrow.*"

We'd made love right there without bothering to go inside.

Only happy, meant-for-each-other couples do that sort of thing, right?

Fast-forward a few years, and he'd had the nerve to paraphrase another line from that favorite book again when we tried to meet civilly to discuss the divorce. With tears in his eyes, he'd said, "These things we do, these choices we make, often lead us to places we'd never intended to go. And I'm broken, and I'm sorry, but the journey to the end can be sweet nonetheless."

Translated: he was sorry.

But not sorry.

Asshole.

Things got less civil after that.

I wonder if I can strap the pergola to the roof of the Acura?

Except for the victorious holes it would leave in the sod, Clay wouldn't mind, even if it hadn't been listed among my assets in the divorce. The happy couple would probably need the room for a swing set or a sandbox anyway. For the baby.

Their baby.

I could steal bungee cords out of the garage.

I needed more wine.

Pushing back from the door casing, I stumbled a half-step. Maybe more wine wasn't the best idea. I had practice the next day, and the team had a strict policy about sobriety on the track. Which, in all honesty, was probably the only thing that saved me from going full-blown Amy Winehouse during my divorce.

Thank God for roller derby.

I also couldn't afford to be sloppy. Not this night. My very last night in the house I'd worked so hard to make a home. Seven years, gone.

"Bodhi!" I whistled, and the dog froze on the grass, letting the tennis ball he'd found drop from his mouth. His big head flopped to the side as he stared at me. "Come on. Let's go inside!"

He picked up the ball again, slung it sideways across the yard, then fetched it.

"Come on, boy!" I slapped the side of my leg, and he ignored me.

The doorbell rang.

Bodhi jerked to attention, then charged, nearly knocking me out of the doorway like a bowling pin. He barked all the way to the door. I followed, depositing my empty glass on the marble countertop with a scraping *clink* as I passed. The bell rang again.

"I'm coming!" I grabbed Bodhi's collar with one hand and pulled open the heavy wood and iron door with the other. It was a vintage piece we'd found in Franklin during the house's remodel.

A party horn sounded in my face, and my friends sang off-key. "Ding! Dong! The jerk is gone! Ding! Dong! The jerk is gone!"

"Oh my god!" I was laughing as

they carried in fuchsia and black balloons, champagne, and a cake. I released Bodhi, letting him sniff and tail-whip my friends who were all in matching black t-shirts with different sayings scrawled in pink.

Monica's shirt: I NEVER LIKED HIM ANYWAY.

Zoey's shirt: SHE'S FREE AT LAST.

Lucy's shirt: GOODBYE, MR. WRONG!

Olivia's shirt: SHE GOT THE RING. HE GOT THE FINGER.

Tears spilled down my cheeks. "You guys!"

"Wait, we have one for you too!" Monica thrust a bright fuchsia shirt toward me.

I held it out as everyone read it

aloud. "We now pronounce you, single and fun!" I pulled it to my chest. "I love you guys."

They all gathered around me for a group hug, Bodhi tangling himself in the middle of our legs. "We love you too," the echoed back.

After a second, Olivia sniffed over my shoulder. "Grace, why does it smell like eggs in this house?"

I wiped my eyes as we all stepped back. "It's a long story."

"And I'm sure it's a great one." Monica held up a bottle. "But first, champagne!"

Lucy grabbed my arm. "No, first Grace has to put on her shirt."

"Yeah, we all changed in the driveway," Olivia agreed.

"OK, OK." I unzipped the Music

City Rollers hoodie I was wearing and slipped the t-shirt over my camisole.

Monica handed me the champagne. "Grace, you do the honors."

Gripping the bottle by its neck, I put both thumbs on the cork and pushed.

Pow!

The cork zoomed across the living room, catching a lampshade and knocking the three-hundred-dollar mouth-blown glass lamp off the end table. It shattered on the floor.

The girls gasped. Bodhi barked and ran a lap around the kitchen island.

Laughing, I handed the bottle back to Monica and grabbed Bodhi's collar as he passed so he wouldn't run through the chards. "Clay got that in the divorce. Oops." They all cackled behind me. "Who's thirsty?"

I let Bodhi back outside, and Olivia helped me sweep up the glass while Monica poured the champagne. When we were finished, Monica held her flute high into the air. "A toast, shall we?"

I smiled and raised my glass with the others.

Monica, my best friend, smiled gently. "To Grace, may this be the beginning of the very best years of your life. I love you."

I mouthed the words "I love you" back to her as everyone shouted, "Cheers!"

Without pause, I drained the champagne, then punctuated the moment with a tiny burp. The girls laughed.

The best years of my life…who

knew I'd be in my thirties before those would roll around.

"Where's your mom? I thought she'd be here." Monica was looking around like she might spot my mother hiding in a corner.

"She offered to come. So did Garrett, but I told them I would be in good hands with you guys."

Lucy sat down at the island in the kitchen. "Who's Garrett?"

"My twin brother," I answered.

"He owns a badass brewery out near Nolensville," Monica added.

"Which one?" Olivia asked as she nosed around my kitchen.

"Battle Road," I answered. "What are you looking for?"

"I serve Battle Road at the restaurant. They have a beer called *Hops on Pops.*" Olivia lifted the lid of the pot on the stove, and her eyes widened as if to say, "*Ah-hah!*" She looked over at me. "Grace, are we dyeing Easter Eggs?"

Not a bad guess, actually.

"Sort of." I joined her at the stove and moved the pot off the burner. "I've decided to have a little fun with that hateful, cheating ex of mine."

Olivia cocked an eyebrow as she sipped her champagne.

"I'm going to write little messages on them and hide them all over the house."

Champagne dribbled down Olivia's chin when she laughed. "That's epic. I want to help."

Zoey gasped and covered her mouth. "You're not really, are you,

Grace?"

Lucy's head tilted toward our friend. "I don't think she's making egg salad, Zo."

I picked up my sewing kit off the floor and plopped it down on the counter. "I'm not just hiding them around the house either. I'll sew them up inside the furniture. That way, when he finds them a few months from now, they'll be nice and ripe with mold and maggots."

Olivia laughed.

Lucy made a vomiting noise.

"Aren't you afraid you'll get into trouble?" Zoey asked.

I patted her head, which was soft with the regrowth of her post-chemo curls. "You gotta live a little, my tiny friend."

Olivia pointed to the mocha-colored sofa. "You could put them in the couch pillows."

Monica walked over and lifted one of the cushions. "No, you need to put them inside the frame so they won't break."

Olivia had evil grin. "Ooo, that's good."

"The only room that's off limits is the nursery." I refilled my champagne one more time. "It's not the kid's fault her parents are assholes."

"Her?" Monica asked.

"Judging from all the Pottery Barn pink in what used to be my home office, it's either a girl or they're really bucking the gender norms."

Monica visibly deflated. Her shoulders sagged, and she lowered her glass down by her thigh. "Grace…"

I aimed the rim of my glass at her, slowly shaking my head with a warning. "Don't. I refuse to be sad."

Monica blinked and forced a fake smile. "I was just going to ask if we can close the windows. It's freezing in here."

God bless her.

In the six months since the bombshell was dropped on our breakfast table in the form of a positive pregnancy test sealed in a sandwich baggie, I'd cycled through a *lot* of emotions. Hatred. Betrayal. Devastation. How could he have done this to us? To *me*? Seven years, and he threw us away. Threw *me* away.

But resentment was the reigning feeling as of late, especially since I was toeing the poverty line. The divorce settlement barely covered the cost of renovating my new home—the tiny apartment above my couture children's boutique, *Sparkled Pink*. And I'd blown my entire life savings on one failed round of IVF. Now Dr. Vagina had the baby *and* my house. Where was the justice in any of that?

"Who wants cake?" Zoey's question snapped me back to the present, and I realized despite Monica's attempt to change the subject, angry tears had pooled in my eyes. I quickly blinked them away before they spilled.

Lucy raised her hand. "Me!"

"Me too," Olivia echoed.

"Me three." I put my glass down on the counter. "I need something to soak up all the booze."

Monica went to where she knew I kept the plates in the cabinet.

Lucy swiveled toward me on her barstool. "Aside from the Easter egg hunt from hell, what's on the agenda this evening?"

Monica handed the plates to Zoey and retrieved a knife from the drawer in the island. "Yeah. Did you say you need to move some more stuff? What's left of yours? You haven't lived here in months."

I sat down beside Lucy. "A box of old college basketball trophies I forgot in the attic, and the rest of the stuff I got in the divorce. The record player and the vinyl collection. The KitchenAid mixer and the velvet Elvis. They're really the only material objects in this den of sin worth fighting for."

"Not the velvet Elvis," Monica said with a laugh.

"Always the velvet Elvis." I smiled and put my hand on Lucy's. "I really just wanted you guys here for moral support."

Lucy smiled. "You've certainly got that."

"Thanks. I know I do." I pointed toward the back door. "I also really want to move the pergola. Think I could strap it to the roof of my car?"

"Jesus, Grace, do you want to go to jail?" Monica asked.

I rolled my eyes. "You're so dramatic. They don't send people to jail for moving pergolas."

"They will when it breaks loose on I-440 and kills a pedestrian!"

"West says we can borrow his truck

if you need to move anything big." Lucy's cheeks flushed at the mention of her new boyfriend's name.

"That's really sweet. Thanks Lucy," I said.

Monica leaned over the bar toward me. "You need to leave the pergola here. I know you love it, but you don't have a yard at your apartment, remember?"

I sighed. "You're right."

"Grace, have you moved into your new place yet?" Olivia asked.

"Last week, actually. It's small, but I like it."

"She really likes not living with her parents anymore," Monica added.

"Definitely. I really appreciate them letting me stay for a while, but it's nice to be back in a home that is mine. And it's even nicer to only have to walk downstairs to go to work."

"I bet," Olivia said. "I keep thinking about doing the same thing at the restaurant, but I'd have to buy the building first."

Olivia owned one of our favorite restaurants in East Nashville, a trendy farm-to-table place called *Lettuce Eat*. The names of her menu items were as creative as the food. My go-to dish lately was the smoked salmon with honey-glazed butternut squash. Or as she called it, *Sofishticated*.

"Check the zoning laws before you build above the restaurant," I warned. "We had to get a special permit."

"Good to know. So you own your building, then?" Olivia asked.

"Sort of." I looked up as Zoey put a

piece of chocolate cake down in front of me. "Thanks, Zo."

"You're welcome, Grace," she said.

I picked up a fork. "My parents own that section of the building. Mom ran a bridal salon out of it before she retired. I'll inherit it someday, but for now, they rent it to me for far less than it's worth."

And I could hardly pay that.

Olivia looked impressed as she picked up a slice of cake. "That's nice."

"It is. Trust me, I know how fortunate I am."

"I need to stop by and see your shop," Lucy said.

Olivia narrowed her eyes. "Why? You're not thinking about babies already, are you?"

"Noooo," Lucy said, dramatically

drawing out the word. "Grace is my friend, and I want to be supportive."

Olivia looked at me. "She's thinking about babies."

I groaned and reached for the champagne bottle again. "Ugh."

"No." Monica snatched the bottle out of my reach. "You've got to drive home sooner or later, and we have practice tomorrow."

I frowned, but I knew she was right.

"Your first practice without me and The Prodigy," Zoey said, smiling at Olivia.

"You can really stop calling me that. The Prodigy wouldn't have been my derby name even if I was playing." Olivia took the champagne and refilled her glass. "And Zoey, you'll make the team on your next go around. We all know you will."

"That's true," I agreed.

Zoey smiled. "I know I'll make it eventually. I won't quit."

I glared at Olivia. "Like *some people.*"

She shrugged. "I was there to help Lucy. She made the team, so mission accomplished."

"We'll really miss skating with you," Monica said.

Lucy wilted in her seat. "Seriously miss you."

"It's not like I won't be involved with the team. You guys will see me the awards thing next month," Olivia said.

My head tilted. "The what?"

"Oh! I forgot to tell you." Monica slapped her own forehead. "The Slammy Awards has been scheduled for the first weekend of December.

Shamrocker told me to tell you we are invited."

"What are the Slammy Awards?" I asked.

"It's the team's annual awards-night celebration," Zoey said.

Monica nodded. "There was a post about it on the app, and I asked Shamrocker if it was open to us newbies too."

"We have an app?" This was all news to me, but to be fair, I'd been so consumed with the finalization of my divorce that I was lucky to have passed my basic skills test.

"I just found out about the awards this week too," Lucy added.

"Are you and West going?"

"Yeah. They do some sort of appreciation thing for all the team sponsors." Lucy's new boyfriend, West Adler, was one of the biggest donors for our team. To say it had caused some drama when they started dating was an understatement.

I wrinkled my nose. "It's a couples thing?"

Monica put her hand on my arm. "If you go, I'll tell Derek to stay at home."

"Aww, Monica." I formed my fingers into the shape of a heart. "Thank you, but Derek should be there. He's sacrificed a lot of time with you for the sake of the sport. It's only right to let him have some fun with it too."

"Are you sure?"

"Positive." I cut another bite of cake with the side of my fork. "Besides, who knows? Maybe I'll ditch my therapist's advice and find myself a date."

Monica smiled. "That's my girl."

"I'll be there too," Zoey added with a bright smile. "I'm volunteering as an NSO, non-skating official, until the next round of Fresh Meat. And they invited all the volunteers."

Lucy clapped her hands. "Yay! The whole group together at derby again."

"Here, here," Olivia said, holding up her glass.

"So you and Styx are good?" I pointed my fork at Olivia. "Things looked a little tense with you two at the Monster's Brawl."

She shrugged. "We're OK now, I think. I got a little too excited that night about seeing an old friend of mine—Hale Damage, your coach for the B-Team."

"You know Hale Damage?" Zoey asked, surprised.

"We went to college together, but we lost touch. I heard she played a while ago, but I didn't know her derby name or that she was still there."

"It didn't come up with you and Styx?" Monica asked. "You've been seeing her for weeks."

Lucy grinned over a bite of cake. "She and Styx haven't done a lot of talking since they've been together."

Olivia pointed at her. "You're one to talk, Miss Screwing Around with a Team Sponsor."

Lucy's cheeks flushed again. "Yeah."

"Anyway," Olivia said, turning back to me. "Haley and I have some *history*, and it didn't go over very well with Styx. We're working through it though."

"Look at you. Not even on the team and still causing shit." I playfully shoved Olivia's arm, but it threw me off-balance on my chair instead. I caught the edge of the countertop and laughed. "Whoa. Yeah, no more booze for me."

Bodhi scratched the back door, and I moved carefully off my stool and across the room to let him back inside. "Good boy," I said, scratching his ear as he trotted through the door.

"Weren't you guys fighting over the dog in the divorce?" Lucy asked. "Who won?"

I scowled and sat cross-legged on the floor with Bodhi. "Clay did." I patted the hardwood and Bodhi flopped down beside me. "Word of advice, if you ever want to have dual ownership of something, don't give it as a gift for a birthday or a holiday. Bodhi was a birthday present."

"Oh, I'm sorry, Grace," Zoey said.

Monica nudged her with her elbow. "Yeah, but Grace's anniversary diamond was also a gift. A two-carat gift."

I raked my nails through Bodhi's fluffy golden fur. "I'd rather have my dog, even if I did sell the ring to pay off my car." I kissed the top of his head and tears threatened to spill again.

"Enough sadness already!" Olivia theatrically gripped the sides of her head. "Geez. I'm going to slit my own wrists over here!"

I cracked a smile and the tingling of

my tear ducts faded.

"She's right." Monica walked over and stood in front of me. "No more tears tonight." She reached down, grabbed both my arms, and hauled me up to my feet. "Come on. This is a party. Let's celebrate by hiding these damn eggs all over the cheating bastard's house and praying for maggots!"

BRITCHES GET STITCHES IS COMING SOON!

Made in the USA
Lexington, KY
02 January 2019